# The Bookie's Daughter

Thomas L. Goodman

This is a work of fiction. All incidents and dialogue, and all characters with the exception of some well-known historical figures, are products of the author's imagination and are not to be construed as real. Where real-life historical persons appear, the situations, incidents, and dialogues concerning those persons are entirely fictional and are not intended to depict actual events or to change the entirely fictional nature of the work. In all other respects, any resemblance to persons living or dead is entirely coincidental.

Table of Contents

# Unbreakable

*Sonia Moravian sat at the kitchen table kneading her rice mix and stuffing her freshly picked grape leaves, listening to the "Armenian station" on the radio. It was Saturday, a day to relax from her nine-to-five secretarial job at the bank. She looked out the window at the budding trees and thought about her mother, Arpine Hagopian, dead two years now, on her would-be birthday. Even more so in death, Arpine Hagopian had remained a mystery, a dark secret.*

*When asked where she was born, Arpine, called "Arpi," would say, "I don't know." When pushed, she'd say, "Aleppo." During her childhood and into her young womanhood and adulthood, Sonia knew very little about her mother. Through hushed conversations, she heard bits and pieces.*

*Over the years, Sonia practically begged her more loquacious Aunt Anna, her mother's sister, to reveal pieces of the family history. Aunty spoke in whispered tones of the torture that she and Arpi had gone through as young women in Armenia and Aleppo, and in between.*

*"Your mother was married before, in Armenia. Her husband was murdered by the Turks," her aunt recounted, swallowing hard, tears rolling down her cheeks." But not before she was pregnant. She lost the baby while she and I "survived" the death marches across the desert to Aleppo. Very few did."*

*"When your mother came to America, she had an arranged marriage with your father, Varkus Hagopian. The matchmaker at the church planned it. Arpine Hagopian knew little English and spoke Armenian when she did speak, which wasn't a lot. But she was a great housewife who did not think about love or intimacy or fun. She dutifully provided for her husband and children."*

*The forced marches of young girls and women through the Syrian desert were part of the planned, systematic genocide specifically calculated by the Turkish Empire to create a pure Muslim-state. The tortured Armenian women as well as the few surviving men, came to the United States scared, angry, and ashamed, but also strong, smart, thankful, and, above all, secretive.*

*Sonia had her own child now, her beautiful son Eddy, her own Armenian community, her own Armenian Apostolic Church, and best of all, her own new granddaughter, Molly. Sonia sat back and envisioned the newborn. She was made of two steel-like materials, the survivorship of not one, but two holocausts. She had been forged with pain and suffering, but also with a maniacal will to endure. "This granddaughter will be strong, brave, smart, but most of all, unbreakable," thought Sonia.*

# Back Rooms

Molly pushed open the heavy silver door at Eddy's Luncheonette and walked in to say hi to her dad. She was tall like her father, had a swimmer's build, and her wavy, shoulder-length black hair was still wet from high school swim practice. She had bright blue eyes, long lashes, and round wire-rimmed glasses when she wasn't wearing her contacts. Most would call her cute. Many would call her beautiful.

The diner was not a fancy place. The counter had ten shiny silver-based stools with bright red vinyl seats that twisted through 360 degrees. There were six booths with seating for four to a table, six in a real squeeze. Molly had been coming to the luncheonette as long as she could remember, by herself or with her dad. Very seldom would she come with her mom. In fact, her mother, Susan, rarely came to the diner at all.

"I don't know what goes on down there. That's your business," she would say to Eddy. Not in an angry or derogatory way, but in a way that said,

"That's nice what you have there. You do what you want. What happens at Eddy's Luncheonette stays at Eddy's Luncheonette."

Molly sat down at the end of the counter. She came straight from swim practice. This year's high school team was undefeated. Molly won some individual events and lost some, but the important thing was that she worked hard to improve. She was glad to be on the team. Swimming was her major diversion from her studies. As a high school senior, she was taking all advanced placement courses and had applied to medical school. Every institution on her list was a six-year program, combining four years of undergraduate studies and four years of medical school into six years.

"Hi, dolly. How are you doing? How was practice?" Eddy was already serving her a tall cup of coffee in a white porcelain mug, extra cream, three artificial sweeteners, a small white plate with two biscotti, one chocolate, one plain. No nuts.

"Thanks, Dad."

As a little girl, her beverage of choice had been hot chocolate with a dollop of fresh whipped cream. She seldom spent time "in the front" unless there were very few customers in the place. Molly heard all sorts of talk from the customers at the counter but never paid much attention to what was said. Most times, she headed for her dad's "office," one of three back rooms.

The first of the rooms was a 10-by-10-foot storage room with a refrigerator, freezer, dishwasher, and dusty shelves filled with bottles of mustard, mayonnaise, ketchup, large containers of cooking oil, loaves of bread, bags of rolls, boxes of napkins, and the usual assortment of dry goods as well as dishes, glassware and cutlery.

The second room was 12-by-12 with a sign on the swinging door that read Employees Only. Entering through that doorway one could see that on the far wall of this second room stood four one-armed bandits. Muted sound. Quarters only.

On the left-hand side of the room, four gray aluminum kitchen chairs rested beside a rustic and scuffed five-by-six-foot solid-oak table in need of refinishing, on top of which sat eight black rotary telephones, their wires snaking back to eight outlets in the baseboard. A wooden box, measuring one-foot cubed with a slit at the top and a metal latch on the side, sat in the center of the table; it seemed poised for something important as it waited there alongside the oversized hard plastic cup that held a dozen or so pens and pencils. A large metal ashtray overflowing with cigarette butts sat off to the right side. A wire wastebasket, always filled to the brim with crumpled papers and discarded brown paper bags, sat on the floor under the table.

On the right-hand wall was a huge Deere and Company safe.

"That's been there before I got here," her father would say when asked. Its worn black exterior made of solid steel had scrolled gold lettering on the door and a large gold-plated combination dial on the front. Standing six feet high, five feet wide, and four feet in length, it weighed over 3,000 pounds.

"There's no way we could ever move that out of here. She's here for life," Eddy would say.

Two or three of her dad's "friends" would sit at the table, answering the phones and smoking cigarettes. They'd remove pieces of white paper from small brown paper bags, scribble on them, and drop the latter into the wooden "drop box." Some men would be yanking at the slot machines. As a little girl, Molly would occasionally peek into this room but she was frightened by the creepy old men and their stinky cigars and cigarettes.

From time to time people would either drop off paper bags at the diner, or runners would collect them from others at their homes or places of work. Inside each bag was a piece of paper with a number on it. The winners matched the lucky number of the day.

Two additional metal fold-out card tables with wooden folding chairs on all sides lined the wall to the right, just inside the doorway where guys like Tommy the Rat, Tony Flowers, Manny the Mule and other guys played pinochle. Glass ashtrays, mugs of coffee, and piles of cash adorned the tables.

The third room, Eddy's office, was the smallest. At the far wall of the room sat a small gray metal desk, a wooden swivel chair on four legs with ball-bearing casters, and a green corduroy seat pad, frayed at the edges. On the desk next to a black rotary telephone and a goose-necked lamp stood a brass-framed picture of Eddy, his wife Susan, his daughter Molly, and his son Leo. A marble-based pen set with two Cross pens sat at the front of the desk with a gold-plated engraving that read: "Be Kind." As a child, Molly spent most of her time there. After school, Molly would come and sit at the desk and do her homework, or read, or simply draw.

"You see, when I first came to New Bedford as a teenager, it was a dump. It had come on hard times and was a shadow of its former self," said Eddy to a wide-eyed daughter, Molly, years ago, during one of their many discussions in the little office.

"Sure, it had its rundown whaling museum and failing aquarium, but by that time it had attracted the worst elements…drugs, the mafia. and God knows what else."

"If you read Moby Dick," he said waving his old copy in front of her, "and if you haven't, you should, Herman Melville in the 1840's described New Bedford as 'thriving and opulent, with grand houses, parks, and gardens.' According to the author, the crews on the whaling ships came from 'all the isles of the sea, and all the ends of the earth.'

"Fact is, you know that Portuguese sweet bread that I serve you in here that you love, well that's a product of the large community of Portuguese people in our town. Those islands were big producers of oranges, like Florida is today. When the industry failed, the islands went to pot. Whalers and their families began to migrate here to make money; they came to New Bedford."

"Even Frederick Douglas came to town in 1838 as a freed slave. He had been a caulker on the docks of the Chesapeake Bay and knew the whaling industry was booming. He too was astonished at 'the wealth and grandeur' of this seaport." But after they struck oil in the States, the whaling boom was ravaged, never to rise again. Just like New Bedford."

As Molly grew older and entered high school, she spent more time sitting at the counter in the diner instead of listening to stories from Eddy. She caught various conversations—about husbands and wives, work, births and deaths, but mostly about the weather, weather, weather, football, football, football, football, or baseball, baseball, baseball.

She occasionally spent time "in that other room" too, in a pinch, when there was a shortage of runners. Once in a while, she would answer the phones, record the bets, and properly arrange the names and numbers. On those days, Molly would check the *Boston Herald* for the attendance at Suffolk Downs that day, note the last three numbers, determine the handle of the day, figure out the take, organize it for her dad, and place the monies due in alphabetical order on his desk.

Over time, Molly transformed her dad's methods. At her suggestion, he had replaced all the big black phones and other old stuff with three internet phones and four laptops. The whole operation was cleaner, faster, more reliable, but most of all, more secure.

Occasionally, for reasons he didn't elaborate, Eddy would ask his daughter to drive over to the houses of people she had known since childhood, like Irene Delgado, Anna Kalafian, or old man Harry Donabedian. She would be politely asked in and given some cookies, *yalanchis* or a piece of paklava. She would invariably leave with a little piece of paper with names and numbers written on it.

Molly's participation was infrequent. Eddy knew his daughter was good with numbers, extremely focused, and trustworthy. Reports from school over the years from her teachers and coaches alike described her as a self-reliant, bright, motivated young lady who had true grit.

Eddy's back-room operation was "a small family business." And he liked it that way. He had roughly a half dozen or so runners. He was always fair, honest, and kind. He did not want any trouble. Hogs go to trough, and pigs go to slaughter, thought Eddy. For certain reasons, some obvious and some not, the police turned a blind eye and the Mob left him alone.

Eddy's favorite was pinball. For this, in the corner to the left, nearest the doorway to the largest room, he placed two pinball machines. No one but no one was as good at pinball as Eddy Moravian. Eddy did not have time nor the inclination for cards, but if anyone ever wanted to challenge him to pinball, they would have to wait in line just after closing, on Wednesdays, and be ready to lose their wad. Nobody beat The Wizard. Nobody.

***

Molly drank her coffee slowly that day and watched her father work the counter and grill. Mostly, he served coffee and pie during these in-between hours of the day. She planned to go home soon to do her homework. Her mom would still be at her one-woman CPA office, where she was CEO, administration, clerical, billing, and accountant all rolled into one. Molly's profile shared features of both her parents: bright, hardworking, strong-willed, honest, and patient to a fault.

Molly got up to leave, but hesitated as she overheard three men at the counter talking softly in commiserating tones.

"Yeah, mom's got cancer too. Turns out that my uncle, aunt, brother, and cousin all got cancer," said one.

"Yeah, same deal happening in my family," said another.

"Sure wish they had a cure for that sucker," said the third.

Molly put on her coat, swung her backpack over her shoulder and said,

"See you at home, Dad."

She walked home thinking about what she had just overheard.

Eddy watched his only daughter, head high and spirits up, as she left the diner. He shook his head. The diner paid their bills and gave his daughter her future. Susan's profession as a tax accountant helped, but the diner was their rock. And although he loved to tell his only daughter about the history of the town, he doubted if he'd ever tell her how he came to own the diner that bore his name.

# Armenian Enclave

Eddy Moravian was not born in New Bedford, though he would live most of his life there. He was raised in Watertown, Massachusetts the largest enclave of Armenians in America. From 1894 to 1924 Turkey carried out the genocide of the Armenian people, but despite documented evidence of the atrocities, the Turkish government to this day denies the existence of a holocaust. In 1939, in a speech laying out the plans for the Final Solution, the extermination of the Jews in Germany and throughout Nazi-occupied Europe, Adolf Hitler asked, "Who, after all, today speaks of the annihilation of the Armenians?"

Eddy's grandparents were from Armenia, Turkey, Iran, and Syria. They survived the Armenian holocaust of the early twentieth century, found their way to America, and made a life for themselves. He knew only smatterings about the latter atrocities, and from an early age he was told never to talk about the Armenian genocide. Never! Not to anyone.

Sonia and Aram, Eddy's parents, grew up and lived in Watertown, met following the Second World War and married soon after. Theirs was a type of arranged marriage. They both came from honest, hardworking immigrant families and could not afford college. Instead, they entered the workforce following high school as they were expected to do. Sonia took advantage of her high school typing course and took a job as a secretary at the bank. Aram took a job at the local New World Market chain that was operated by its founder, a favorite Armenian son from Watertown.

Aram was a loving, forgiving father and husband. Grateful for what he had. He was tall, handsome, and athletic. Some would say powerful. A gentle giant of sorts. The one piece of advice he would always give to Eddy went something like this,

"When you have a problem, you gotta look at it frontwards, backwards, and sideways. Then lead with your left."

Aram's true love was playing the oud, a tear-drop shaped mandolin-like stringed instrument with a deep rounded back, which he played for years at Armenian events to make extra pocket change.

As a youngster, Eddy was well read and his teachers praised him for his breadth of knowledge. They lauded his uncanny mathematics abilities. He was known to be a dutiful kid who stayed out of trouble. Quiet. He got along with everybody. Above all, "kind" was the word consistently used by those who knew him.

Sonia, Eddy's mother, kept to herself. She was a reserved woman who emoted little, but was a loving, caring mother and wife. She spoke little of herself or her family's past. She not only worked hard at keeping a clean home for her small family but was always the first to roll up her sleeves at the church bazaars and for all the Armenian charity drives.

Eddy's most vivid childhood memories were the aromas coming from his mother's kitchen. Always using the freshest ingredients, his mother grew her own grape leaves in their small backyard and taught him how to know when they had reached peak ripeness and were ready to harvest. She would teach him how to roll her herbed rice mix into the brined grape leaves to form the *yalanchis* that he adored. Long after his youth was a distant memory, just the thought of Armenian delicacies such as *sujuk* (spicy sausage), *lahmajoun* (thin baked round bread topped with spiced meat and herbs), *bulgar* (a whole grain most often made from cracked parboiled durum wheat), and *choerag* (twisted buns of sweet bread) could still make his mouth water. Of course, his favorite was Armenian *paklava*, a multilayered pastry made with phyllo and layered with crushed nuts, honey, butter, sugar, and cinnamon. This ancient cuisine dates back to 900 BC, so long ago that many archaeologists and religious historians believe that Noah's Ark came to rest in the "land of Mount Ararat" (Armenia).

Then there was lamb: lamb kabobs, lamb chops, fried lamb, stewed lamb shanks, roast leg of lamb, rack of lamb, filet of lamb, lamb with vegetables, curried lamb, and on and on. Too much! So much so that as he grew older, Eddy couldn't stand to look at lamb.

* * *

The Armenian Apostolic Church is the face of Armenian Christianity that brought the wrath of the Turkish government to murder two million Armenians (along with any and all persons of the Christian faith) during the first quarter of the twentieth century. St. Didikian's was one of four Armenian churches in Watertown.

An Armenian priest is allowed to be married before ordination. Such a married priest is known as a kahana. Like most of his generation, Kahana Harut Azekian of St. Didikian's had a certain anger, shame, and sternness to his demeanor. All the children of his congregation, including Eddy, knew to stay clear of Kahana's crosshairs.

Harut Azekian was paid a meager salary. He was dedicated to his flock and was glad to be in a community surrounded by his kind. His teenage son, Gregory, did not appreciate the finer points of being the son of a kahana. Outside of school, Gregory's major activities had always been paired with church activities, helping his father prepare for one church related event or another. His social life was confined to the church picnic and the church bazaar; weddings, baptisms, funerals, and the Christmas and Easter holidays events. He was jealous of the other kids: their activities, their possessions, their freedom.

By the time he was in high school, Gregory Azekian realized that this was not the life he wanted to lead. The other kids noticed an angry edge to him, but none of them, particularly the Armenian kids, wanted to get on the bad side of Kahana or his son. Gregory became a bully of sorts.

As Gregory's senior year rolled around, he began targeting Paulie Viola, Eddy's best friend, for no clear reason. He began by spreading nasty rumors about Paulie. Then, he vandalized Paulie's mom's car one day when she let her son take it to school. Next, he snuck a bottle of liquor into Paulie's locker and proceeded to inform the principal. Maybe Gregory was mad about Paulie going out with his sister. Or maybe he was angry that this Italian kid always seemed to have money, thanks to the extra cash Paulie made from his after-school job at Star Market that he took to help out his mom. Or maybe he was pissed that his sister seemed to enjoy herself while smoking in the parking lot after school with her boyfriend before the latter went to work.

Smoking cigarettes on the sly was a pleasure that Eddy and Paulie enjoyed when they got a chance to hang out together. They would often take a ride to Turner Hospital, a private psychiatric hospital built on a beautiful forty-acre setting of forests, gardens, lawns, and circular roadways, with trails meandering through the woods. As a freshman, Eddy ran through the wooded trails as a member of his high school cross-country team. The woods were composed of century-old oaks, birches, maples, and Dutch Elm. Some were over 200 feet tall and three to four feet in diameter. The forests had not been culled in years. Many of the Dutch elm had succumbed to Dutch elm disease where they began to rot from the inside out.

On a spring evening in their senior year, Paulie borrowed his mother's car and picked up Eddy. They took a drive to Turner Hospital grounds and cruised in the Subaru, smoking and talking and just hanging out. They parked the car near the rose garden, got out, and leaned against the car in the cool, quiet dusk, blowing smoke rings and French inhaling.

Suddenly, a blue Honda pulled up, screeched to a halt, and out stepped Gregory Azekian.

"Hey Paulie, you think you're such a lover boy? You think you can manhandle my sister?"

Paulie stared down at his feet, ears turning red, trying to ignore Gregory.

"How 'bout I tell my old man that you knocked up my sister, huh? How 'bout that?" He rummaged in his back pocket and pulled out a knife. Paulie looked up, eyes focused on the four-inch ivory base made of gold, turquoise, and silver with inlaid abalone. Gregory pushed a button on the side of the handle and a six-inch blade snapped out, stiletto style. He came closer, pointing the knife in Paulie's face.

"Hey, Paulie, how 'bout you hand over all the money in that fat wallet of yours, asshole?"

Suddenly, Paulie flipped his cigarette at Gregory's face, shouting, "Fuck you!" Feeling equally scared and triumphant as the lit cigarette caught Gregory in the right eye, Paulie yelled, "Get in the car. Hurry!"

"You fucking…" shouted Gregory. Eddy's eyes were like saucers. His heart thumped hard in his chest. He flung open the car door without thinking.

The two friends jumped in the car, Paulie revved the engine, and they sped off with Gregory in hot pursuit. As they raced around the winding roadways at breakneck speed in the dark, neither of them said a word. They were not sure how crazy Gregory was or could be as he sped closer and closer.

"Take a left here," Eddy suddenly screamed, pointing to a barely visible dirt road with scarcely room for one car. Paulie followed Eddy's direction. He was blinded by Greg's high beams glaring in his rearview mirror. Eddy knew every road and trail on the property from his cross-country days. Soon Eddy yelled again, "Quick, take a sharp right between those two trees," pointing down an even murkier lane. Paulie jerked the steering wheel to the right.

The blazing headlights disappeared. Gregory missed the turn. With an ear-splitting *bang*, his car smashed into a huge old elm tree that cracked and folded at the point of impact. The remainder of the tree came crashing down on the roof of Gregory's car, crushing it as one would crumple a piece of tin foil for discard. Paulie slowed the car to a crawl. The two boys stared at each other in silence. Both had their mouths wide open, brows furrowed and their chins stretched down to their chests. "Holy fuck!" whispered Eddy.

Not another word was spoken between them. Paulie backed up cautiously and slowly drove away. Eddy had trouble breathing. Paulie thought his heart was going to pump through his chest. In silence, he pulled into Eddy's driveway and dropped him off at the front door to his house. Pale as a snow leopard and with trembling hands that could barely hold onto the steering wheel, Pauli drove home and wearily pulled the car into his mother's driveway.

The next day, the two friends decided together that it would be best if they left Watertown as soon as possible. Paulie Viola heard about jobs for textile salesmen in New Bedford, so they made plans to leave home after graduation. Paulie's father, Nicky Viola, had left home when his son was twelve and now owned and ran Nick's Diner in the heart of downtown New Bedford. The boys planned on living with him.

# Squeezed

Nicky Viola's hands trembled as he wiped down the counter at Nick's Diner in the heart of downtown New Bedford. He had a burning ache in his stomach, a tightness in his chest, a numbness in his digits. One little mistake.

Fingers Filano, head of the Cosa Nostra in southern Massachusetts, ran the rackets and extortions in New Bedford including the numbers in the back of Nick's Diner. Not long ago, Nicky "threw in a few dollars." He had gotten a tip. He just wanted to surprise his son with a used car, as a thank you. Even though Paulie and Eddy covered a large catchment area as New England textile salesmen, they worked hard in their spare time filling in at the diner when Nicky needed them. It was a sure thing. Until it wasn't. He lost—big time. He now owed Fingers $5,000.

Nicky did not have that kind of money, but Fingers would not let him off the hook. Fingers is either going to kill me, take away the diner, or both, thought Nicky.

The gangster's abusive taunting started off slowly, with Fingers coming around to the diner more often. His demands continued. Fingers would not let up.

"How 'bout a glass of wine, Nicky," grunted Fingers.

"You know we don't serve wine here, Mr. Filano," Nicky said sheepishly. "It's against the law."

Moishie Stein, Fingers' second-in-command, turned his attention to Nicky.

"Hey, why don't you give him some of that red wine you got stashed in the back. Fingers might like you better."

Recently a case of Chianti showed up anonymously at Christmastime for Eddy. "For being a good kid," read the attached note. Nick told Eddy to place it in the back next to the cases of coffee.

Fingers would not let up. Nicky told Eddy to go in the back and pop one of the bottles of Chianti and serve it in the only wine glass they had. The glass had come as part of a holiday gift package of a glass and some cheap wine Nicky re-gifted to Sergeant Bobby Brown last Christmas. Nicky kept the glass.

Moishie Stein said to Fingers, "Hey, why don't you go easy on the guy? It's only five Gs."

Fingers replied, "Ay, it's not the coin. It's the principle of the thing. You let one guy go, and they all think they can get away with whatever. I got a reputation!"

"Hey, Nicky we gotta' work somethin' out here. You owe me five big ones. You gotta' pay. I don't want to have to take the diner away from you. Or worse."

"Let it go, Frankie (Fingers' real name). He's got his son in here, who's a good kid. And he's got that Armenian kid who always treats you good, Boss."

Moishie continued, "This is your place. You come in here three, four, five days a week. Every week. He gives you free food, and you're the only guy in here he serves wine to. It's all on the house. And he ain't even got a liquor license."

But Fingers had been stiffed. By his very nature, he could not let Nicky go unpunished. He would make him pay.

Within a month, Fingers had his guys deliver four one-armed bandits to the back room.

"Eighty-twenty. You'll earn your nut," growled Fingers.

Nicky was stuck. He could not afford to lose the diner. He had hoped to make a buck or two and then leave the diner to Paulie. After his marriage went sour, and he became estranged from the rest of his family, Paulie and the diner were the only things he had.

"I just don't know what the hell to do," he fretted to his son.

Karen Isopo was a nurse on the pediatric wards at New Bedford General Hospital. She often worked with children with behavioral problems. Some had severe anxiety or depression or attention deficit disorder (ADD), or perhaps attention deficit hyperactivity disorder (ADHD). Some of the latter children were on Adderall or Ritalin, medications that were designed to help these patients focus and direct their energy in a positive way.

Karen did not feel guilty about "borrowing" some of their medicine at times. As she would distribute their medication on morning rounds, she would simply slip one of the two pills prescribed into the pocket of her clean, crisp, white nurse's uniform.

Among Karen's other duties at the hospital were morning blood draws. Karen did not mind drawing blood and starting I.V.s because this helped to hone her skills for the job she would soon be starting as an oncology nurse at a private cancer center in town.

"You have Fingers Filano today," a fellow nurse said. "He is head of the local Mafia, a three-pack-per-day smoker, and drinks like a fish. He always gets himself admitted to the hospital just as he is about to go on trial. He fakes a heart attack and stays "until the wind dies down." Rumor had it that people assigned to draw his blood did a lot of shaking.

The patient was tall and slender, with steely blue-gray eyes, and thinning salt and pepper hair combed straight back. He smirked at Karen and stuck out his arm. Karen proceeded to draw his bloodwork with a calm, self-assured technique. As she collected the vials of blood, Karen felt a hard pinch on her right buttock.

Karen turned quickly and stabbed his hand with the needle.

"Is that why they call you 'Fingers'?" she snapped. "You ever do that again and I will report you to the chief of medicine, head of nursing, and the board of directors."

Frank sat up in bed, gave Karen a menacing look, and sighed,

"Nobody's reportin' nobody to nobody." He held up his right hand, revealing two stubs where the fourth and fifth digits should have been. "Years ago, some lady took a swipe at me with a real sharp knife and missed what she was going for. Luckily, she only got two fingers."

* * *

Paulie Viola first met Karen when she was the nurse at New Bedford Hematology/Oncology, P.C.. She drew his blood after his general practitioner told him he was pale and asked him to get checked for anemia. Paulie failed to tell his doctor about his sleepless nights, how he felt jittery, anxious, and how he was worried about his dad. He followed up with the hematologist who told him that the blood Karen drew was normal and his hemoglobin count was fine. He did not have anemia.

He did, however, wait for Karen after work and asked her out for a cup of coffee. He felt proud to take her to the diner where he worked alongside his father. The couple spent time with one another on several more occasions between their work schedules, and as they talked and got to know each other Paulie found out about Karen's grandfather's terminal illness.

"I'm sorry about your grandfather. How are you and your parents holding up?" said Paulie with a sympathetic smile.

"Thanks. We've known this was coming," said Karen with tears in her eyes. "Why don't you stop by the house after work?"

Karen lived with her parents and on a subsequent evening Paulie came to pay a visit, bouquet in hand. He paid his respects to her parents with a homemade ricotta pie from the diner. Paulie and Karen talked and walked around the neighborhood and while light snow fell throughout the evening and night.

Paulie told Karen practically his entire life story, including how his father was in a lot of trouble, in debt to Fingers Filano for more money than he could afford. How he could lose the diner. Karen relayed the abusive episode she had experienced with Fingers Filano in the hospital. On that night and during the several weeks to follow, Karen and Paulie devised a plan.

***

On the second Tuesday that January, several weeks after her grandfather died, Karen punched in the code and let herself in to the office, an hour before others were scheduled to arrive. Her hands were shaking as she turned on the lights, took off her coat, hat, mittens, and boots, slipped into her clogs, and heaved her backpack upon her shoulders as she made her way to the supply room. Once there, she quickly took the thirty small bottles of chemotherapy marked Cyclophosphamide off the shelf and placed them on the nearby table. Her breathing was rapid.

Karen carefully opened each box, removed the bottles, each containing forty white chemotherapy pills, unscrewed each cap, and emptied the contents of each bottle into an eight-by-six-by-four-inch Tupperware container. The package insert within each box of pills listed the possible side effects including nausea, abdominal pain, diarrhea, hair loss, mouth sores, fever, chills, and hemorrhagic cystitis. The latter condition often caused inflammation and severe bleeding of the bladder, resulting in painful, often uncontrolled bloody urination.

She then took the thirty bottles of look-alike pills she had bought at the pharmacy, removed them from their bottles, and filled each empty chemotherapy bottle with exactly forty impostor pills.

She was just about finished when Nancy Spencer, her head nurse, arrived at work on that snowy day.

* * *

Nancy Spencer, the head oncology nurse at New Bedford Community Oncology Practice, P.C. was never late. Well, almost never. She had been working as the head oncology nurse at the same practice for 30 years. As doctors and nurses and receptionists came

22

and went, Nancy remained a constant … rock solid. Those who knew her would invariably say, "When Nancy was created, they broke the mold."

"Good morning, Karen," she said. "Sorry I'm late, but it looks like you have everything in perfect shape, as usual."

"Yeah, I got in early," Karen said with a smile. "Paulie dropped me off on his way to work."

Karen Isopo had only been working with Nancy for six months, but thus far, she had proven to be a great asset to the practice. She was a quick learner, good with patients, and got along with those in the office.

"I remember now," Nancy said. "We were going to go over inventory today. The shelves look spick-and-span. Thanks."

Nancy looked over the supplies. Karen had wiped off all the shelves and arranged all the supplies in neat order with the most-used items easiest to access. A large assortment of tools of the trade—intravenous tubing, various sizes of needles and syringes, masks, paper gowns, latex gloves, bottles of betadine, medical-grade alcohol wipes, and multiple shelves filled with stand-alone vials, as well as boxes of medications, mostly chemotherapy—lined the shelves. A very close look would have revealed that one section where thirty small boxes of pills once stood was especially clean and orderly.

"Well, let's have a go at the inventory," said Nancy. "We might have a chance to take a real bite out of it before the first patients come in."

When Nancy came to the boxes of Cyclophosphamide she examined the labels and said,

"These are so old. We haven't had any patients who have required Cyclophosphamide in a while. These pills are probably out of date."

Karen felt her face get a little flushed. Her heart was racing. She knew she had to stay calm. As Nancy began to open a box, Karen said,

"I think the outdate is right on the side of the box."

Nancy twisted the box in her hand and squinted at the tiny writing.

"Oh yeah. Here it is. It says to discard after October of last year—three months ago. But if we send it back to the distributor, we may be able to get a refund."

Karen drew in a sharp breath. She forced herself to stay calm. She struggled to focus and stay on point while they completed the task at hand. Next, the two oncology nurses put their findings into the computer.

"Great job, Karen," Nancy said. "I'll email Empire, the distributor, and see what they can do for us."

# Cause of Death

About a month after the inventory, Nancy stopped Karen just outside the chemotherapy room.

"I'm headed to give a patient an injection, but I want to talk to you about those bottles of Cyclophosphamide."

Karen's heart sank. She could barely think.

"Oh, I thought you said to throw them away," said Karen in what she hoped was a casual tone. "So, I did, into the hazardous-waste bin."

Nancy looked Karen straight in the eyes and said slowly,

"I didn't tell you to throw them away."

"Oh, you didn't?" asked Karen, grimacing while her chest tightened. "I'm sorry."

A long moment of silence hung in the air between the two as Nancy studied Karen. Karen flashed back to her childhood when her mother caught her with her hand in her purse, trying to steal a few dollars.

"That's all right. Neither the distributor nor the manufacturer would give us a refund. I was just coming over to throw the pills away. You did me a favor. Thanks."

* * *


Fingers Filano hadn't been feeling well for weeks. Between intermittent nausea and off-and-on stomachaches, he was miserable. The pain was more like what some of his girlfriends described as cramping, just above his pubic bone. He was drinking bottles of Pepto Bismol, but the stuff didn't seem to help.

On top of that, when he went to take a piss one day, pure blood came out. "What the fuck?" This had been going on for over a month. No way he was telling anyone. Maybe it was an infection? Or maybe it was his prostate? He knew a guy who had kidney stones. Could it be cancer?

Fingers needed a change of scene.

Accompanied by Moishie Stein, Fingers walked into the diner around 4 p.m. and sat down in one of the booths. Without a word, Paulie served him his usual glass of Chianti. Nicky was out at a doctor's appointment, so Paulie and Eddy were manning the diner.

Over the last several months, each time Fingers came into the diner, no matter the hour, Paulie or Eddy would dole out a teaspoonful of the white, odorless powder furnished by Karen into a wine glass, pour the wine, stir it vigorously, and serve it to Mr. Filano.

"Hey, I want a glass of wine, too," other customers would demand." "I'm sorry, we don't serve alcohol here," Nicky, Paulie, or Eddy would reply.

When he finished his dinner that evening, Fingers got up from the booth, staggered a bit, and fell to the floor.

"Fingers!" yelled Moishie. No response. Moishie yelled louder, "Call 911."

Against his groggy objections, the ambulance crew helped Fingers into the van. On the ride to the emergency room, the paramedics commented that the patient was pale, had labored breathing, and complained of lower abdominal, chest, and left arm pain. They also noticed the large stain at the front of his pants that seemed to spread out from his zipper.

"Urine," announced the junior paramedic, but on closer inspection of the bright red stains on the sheets beneath Fingers, that pronouncement changed to "Blood! He's bleeding."

Lying half-unconscious on the gurney in the ER, Frank heard the urologist introduce himself as Dr. Mathew Perrino.

"Frank?"

Dr. Perrino's voice in his ear brought Frank around, and he instantly felt pressing pain in his chest.

"Frank, you are losing a lot of blood and your red blood count is dangerously low."

Frank moaned and tried to speak, but all that came out was "Chest."

"Your oxygen level is extremely low as well; you're on supplemental oxygen now, so you should start to feel better soon," said a nurse.

Before anyone could stop him, Frank yanked out his urinary catheter, screaming as he did so, causing him to bleed all the more. He collapsed back down on the stretcher, moaning.

"Mr. Filano, in order to diagnose you properly, I have to insert a scope into your bladder to see what is going on in there. It will be uncomfortable but I will try to make it brief. I will take a quick look and will then remove the scope."

As the doctor began to insert the metal scope into Frank's penis, pushing up into the bladder, monitor alarms sounded to alert a full-blown cardiopulmonary arrest.

The emergency room filled with renewed urgency as the team tried medications, shock paddles juiced up to their highest level, blood transfusions and emergency injections to revive the patient, but Fingers Filano could not be resuscitated. Time of death was called at 7:20 p.m.

***

As they walked out of the back door to St. Francis of Assisi Church following Fingers' funeral, Nicky, Paulie, and Eddy lit their cigarettes. Nicky signaled toward the street with a nod, and the three strolled down the sidewalk together. After a block or so, Nicky slowed down and stopped.

He turned to Eddy and said,

"Look, Eddy. Thanks for what you did. No choice, I guess. You have been good friends with my son for a long time. You've been a great kid, worked hard at the diner, and never caused any problems." Nicky stopped to take a long drag of his cigarette.

"There's been some talk around town. Paulie did give him that last glass of wine. I heard some guys say something about poisoning Fingers. Rick Stillano came by the diner and said he had a message from Moishie Stein. It would be best if Paulie and I skipped town for a while. Indefinite."

Nicky hesitated for a moment and then uttered abruptly,

"I want you to take the diner. You're what, 25? You can handle it. I'll get you all the papers. No strings. You run it until we get back. Not sure when that will be. Maybe you can bank me five percent of the take. I can send you word where we are at some point."

Nicky's voice cracked at "some point."

"Thanks for all your help. You've been like a son to me …" His voice trailed off.

"We should get going." Eddy felt uncomfortable at that point asking whether Karen would be leaving town with them.

Nicky put a key in Eddy's palm. The three men all shook hands, then exchanged hugs and "Good luck" all around.

"Take care of yourself," Paulie said. Father and son turned and walked away, disappearing down the street. He never saw them or Karen again.

***

Eddy was stunned by the sudden change in events, this gift he had just been handed. Still in shock, he sat at a diner table and flipped through the *Daily Gazette* absentmindedly. Suddenly the bell on the diner door tinkled.

"Whaddya doin' kid, daydreamin? Give a guy a cup of coffee, goddammit," snapped Moishie Stein. The tough guy had walked in on Eddy while his head was in the clouds. They called Stein "the Jew." He was maybe five feet, nine inches tall, weighed maybe 180–190, but you could tell he was solid and could really pack a punch.

Eddy served up the coffee, then went behind the counter. He surreptitiously stared at his only customer. One might be tempted to call Moishie "in good shape," but he loved to eat and drink, loved his cigars, and had a double chin. His favorite meal was pickled herring for an appetizer, a big bowl of borscht with a dollop of sour cream for

28

his entrée, a warm bialy to go with it, and a large piece of halvah for dessert.

Moishie rose high up in the ranks, mainly as a bagman at first, but he knew how to keep his mouth shut. He was smart. He was a good reader of character. No one pulled the wool over Moishie's eyes. Fingers liked having him around as his number-two man. The funny thing was, Moishie had a good heart.

When Moishie got off his counter stool to leave the diner, he left a big tip.

"Don't worry, kid, you'll do all right—I got my eye on you." He flashed a half smile, showing off his gold-capped tooth on the second right molar.

Nonetheless, Eddy was unable to sleep that night.

# Survivor

Molly loved to read as long as she could remember, ever since her parents began taking her to the New Bedford Public Library every week to check out and return books. The town library was a marvelous structure built of Massachusetts field stones, cleared from the rocky fields by the New England farmers. These rounded stones of all sizes, from that of an orange to the size of a watermelon, were not only used to build the never-ending New England property walls but were used to construct the three-turreted New Bedford library.

It was a massive structure with the middle turret being the tallest, each tower topped by a conical, slated roof. The entrance consisted of two enormous oak doors. Each door had three large black metal hinges and was adorned with nine black iron studs, three across and three down. The wrought iron handles were huge and black, and no child could resist trying to push the latch and heave the door open with all their might to view the huge entryway to the "castle". Above the doorway, etched into the stone lintel, read, "The Sea is Our Home. God Watches O'er".

The library was made of three canyon-like rooms such that when you entered, your footsteps would echo throughout the building. One had to walk softly, perhaps on tip-toes, in order not to disturb the other readers. Each room had twenty-foot ceilings with stacks of books that reached to the crown molding. Huge oil paintings of whaling ships sporting ornate gold leaf frames, hung on the expansive stone walls. Each had an oval-shaped, gold plaque at the bottom center, naming the pictured ship and the years it spent at sea. And what made this library even more magical?

On the far wall of each room was a wrought iron spiral staircase, wedged between the panoply of books plastering the walls. The winding staircases rose to the ceiling, and as one reached the top of each, there was a four-foot by one-foot window wedged between the stacks that allowed an individual three different viewpoints of New

Bedford harbor. The stairwells were most often roped off with signs saying," No entrance. Please refer questions to the librarian." But on special days of the year, children of certain ages were allowed to climb the stairs, accompanied by an adult. Molly would climb the stairs and look out as often as she could. This fortress of information was Molly's sanctuary.

On one such trip to the library, when she was nine years old, she picked out a little book called The Way the World Began. Now of course, she had been told over and over again in Sunday school how God had created the earth in seven days (actually, in six days and rested on the seventh). From the first to the last page of this new book, Molly was horrified, awestruck, curious, confused, scared and fascinated. What was this book saying? Galactic explosions, atoms, molecules, chemicals, proteins, one-cell organisms going to two, then four, then eight in a sea of cells, then fish, then amphibians, then amphibians able to crawl on land, then land animals, then dinosaurs? Were she and the author the only ones that knew about this? Suppose other people found out? She would keep this secret to herself for now.

She proceeded to exhaust the New Bedford Public Library of books related to science and chemistry and natural history. She soon realized she needed more resources than her bygone hometown library could provide. Molly knew at an early age what she wanted. She needed bigger and better.

One hundred and fifty years had taken its toll on the now downtrodden city of New Bedford. Who would have guessed that the next New Bedford boom would be one of brilliance? Who knew there would emerge a young star destined to put the sheen back on that crummy old seaport?

* * *

Swimming came naturally to Molly. She practically learned to swim before she could walk. She felt so comfortable in the water. Her

31

strokes were effortless. She could swim any stroke, but the American crawl was her forte.

Susan would take Molly And her brother Leo to Horseneck Beach in the summer. Located on the Massachusetts-Rhode Island border, it boasted white sand dunes studded with seagrasses, surrounded by stretches of meandering ocean roses. Molly remembered the ocean sparkled so intensely as the July and August sun bounced off its waves. But the Massachusetts coastal waters were not warm, even in the summer—maybe 70 degrees.

Eddy was usually working. The three would spend the day swimming or walking the beach collecting shells. They'd picnic on their king-size blue blanket, their large red and black plaid thermos always filled with pink lemonade. Susan would call them out of the water,

"Come meine liebe Kinder. Come sit next to me and have your lunch."

Her mother, who was an excellent swimmer, would freestyle her way from buoy to buoy, while the two siblings body-surfed in the tides. Sometimes, their *Bubbe* (grandmother) Sadie Bloom, would come with them. Now, if you really wanted to see perfection in the water, that's who you'd want to study. *Bubbe* Bloom had a figure like a woman twenty years her junior, and her swim strokes were smooth as glass. If asked, she would quietly say in her German accent that she "learned in the old country."

As for her high school swim team, Molly looked forward to practices as much, if not more, than swim meets. She liked pushing herself, and her times reflected her consistent improvement over the last few years. She swam the 400-meter freestyle and was third in the freestyle relay. The daily workout gave her and her teammates a chance to physically, emotionally, and psychologically chill. It helped most of them to better focus on their studying at night.

The swim team had been a great way to meet other kids. Kitty McKee was her best friend. The best swimmer on the team, Kitty, was a born athlete. She was tall, trim, muscular, with long blonde hair, and bright, emerald-green eyes. She was street-smart and gutsy.

No one would call her the studious, bookworm type. She had a sixth sense, though, about people's natures, their bents, their tendencies, their intentions. She was a loyal, trustworthy, and spirited friend, totally devoid of BS.

The two best friends hung out both in and out of school. While Molly enjoyed the science club, chess club, and math society, Kitty excelled on the soccer field, swim team, and softball diamond. With schoolwork, and extracurricular activities neither girl had a robust social life.

Molly dated here and there but nothing stuck. Both girls respected each other for their talents, their opinions and sensitivities, but most of all, their cherished friendship.

In a way, the two young women could not be more dissimilar. With Molly's parents always working, and Kitty's mother enduring the struggles of being a single mom, the two cronies hung out several days a week after swim practice.

"Intoxicating" was the word that the two friends chose to describe the feeling they had when immersed in the cold water, focusing as they swam their quota of 80, 90, 100 laps per day. Kitty was driven. There was no athletic move that she could not master. As for Molly, she did her best thinking when she swam her laps. Interestingly, when Molly was asked how she got to be such a good swimmer, she would simply say with pride, "Runs in the family."

Both excelled in their own realms, but Molly's motivation came from positive nurturing, while Kitty's drive sprang from her drive to get away from her home environment and to succeed despite it all. A lifelong trust emerged as they survived teenage relationship successes and defeats, or the time they got caught smoking their first cigarettes, or their first sampling from Kitty's mother's liquor cabinet, or when they were grounded for taking the family car for a drive around town when neither had their license.

Molly would always sit up front for Kitty's first place athletic presentations. Kitty was front row and center for Molly's science award ceremonies.

At swim meets, as she watched Molly excel, Susan often thought back to her own mother and what swimming meant to her.

* * *

In July 1943, Allied bombers targeted Hamburg, Germany aiming to destroy the port city's oil refineries, shipyards, and U-boat pens. The destruction wrought by Operation Gomorrah claimed 37,000 civilian lives and utterly decimated the city of Hamburg.

On the last Sunday of that month, Franciscan Brother Josef Zeitzmann of St. Johannes Church in Hamburg heard the cries of a child somewhere nearby. He had just crawled up the wooden stairs and out of the trap door leading to the church basement. He latched the barely visible, heavy, wooden escape hatch, and covered it over with the eight-by-ten-foot Turkish carpet.

He thought he heard whimpering from where the confession booth stood before the bombing. As he grew closer to the sound, he saw a young child huddled in the corner, perhaps ten years old, with bright blue eyes wearing a tan "car coat" with an argyle scarf, and a yellow Star of David sewn to the right sleeve of her coat. Her jaw-length black hair framed a face begrimed with black soot. Tears tracked down her cheeks, dripping from her nose and chin. She wore scuffed, black ankle boots that had pointed toes, along with dirty white ankle socks. A small gold chain embraced her right ankle from which hung a small heart-shaped locket.

Half the church had been destroyed by Allied bombings. The altar, the pulpit, and three-quarters of the pews were obliterated. The darkened sky loomed over the sacred edifice through a huge, gaping hole in the roof. The large crucifix on the eastern wall that had once been the beacon for congregants within, now swung from a single black wire. The stained-glass windows on either side of the nave were cracked, broken, or gone entirely.

Brother Josef approached the girl carefully, slowly, and sitting down on the ground a few feet away, put on his kindest, most empathetic expression. He sat there silently for some thirty minutes, making no demands, no movement, despite the fact that he knew time was of the essence. Much had to be arranged, and quickly… proper papers, change of clothes, transportation, phone calls, and go-betweens. Though he said nothing, he was planning how to get this child to Sister Lieband at St. Georg's nunnery in Rosengarten, a small town just outside of Hamburg. He knew the child would never see her parents again. The only remembrance of them would be the photograph inside the small gold charm on her right ankle. She would never take it off.

***

The first time the nuns at St. Georg's took Klara Helschwamann (aka Sadie Levine) to the lake to swim with the rest of the children, they marveled at her remarkable strokes. They sent her to a local pool for lessons, and she was soon accepted into the Hamburg Swim Club. Klara became a phenom. She worked hard in the pool for the city-state of Hamburg and Lower Saxony. She was soon chosen to train for the next Olympic games, making her a member of the elite.

The German government took their Olympic athletes very seriously, particularly their swimmers. Years later, in the 1960s, East Germany began a decades-long government-sponsored program, Der Leistungssportbeschluss, where it secretly gave their swimmers and other Olympic athletes performance-enhancing anabolic steroids. But back then, Klara just swam her head off.

Of course, things were always a bit shaky at the nunnery with German SS officers searching from time to time for Jewish and Gypsy children, or children who were mentally or physically slow. Throughout the war, the nuns and children would persistently be tortured with this terror-stricken game of hide and seek with the Gestapo.

Following the 1936 Games in Berlin, no Olympic games were held in 1940 or 1944. Not until 1948 in London were the Olympic Games recommenced following WWII. As the war wound down and Germany was defeated, children like Klara were brought to the United States and adopted into a home through Catholic Charities.

And so, Klara Helschwamann was adopted by a hardworking Catholic couple who were unable to have children of their own and finished her high school years at New Bedford High. Following her graduation, she got a job as an assistant to a local apparel manufacturer, Julius Bloom.

During WWII, Julius's German parents with their infant son escaped extermination in Nazi-occupied Europe by moving constantly, hiding in a different home, basement, attic every few days if necessary, for years, in order to stay ahead of the unrelenting Nazi "search" parties. Eventually they were able to stow away on a boat bound for Argentina. From there they meandered their way to the United States, finally disembarking a ship in Boston Harbor. Julius' father, Irving, went on to found a textile printing firm, which Julius had recently taken over. This was located at the North End of New Bedford, the Jewish community centered around Temple Emmauel.

Bloom Textile Printing Company, a once successful enterprise with a multitude of national accounts, was failing before Julius took the helm. The textile manufacturing industry in the Northeast had finally succumbed to cheaper products from the South.

Julius did an about face, recruited artists and designers, revamped his factory's machinery, and began producing, marketing, and selling men's casual wear for the "Modern Gentleman." His very first hire was a personal assistant, a shy, intelligent young lady with a German accent, Klara Helshwammann.

Klara and Julius were attracted to each other from the start. While at first everything between them was pure business, their relationship became personal very quickly. His bright-eyed, athletic assistant who helped him launch his new business venture, Bloom's Apparel, was the girl of his dreams. Within six months Julius Bloom brought Klara home to introduce her to his parents. He announced his intentions to his parents.

"Not on your life!" his mother yelled. "Absolutely not!"

"Over our dead bodies," shouted his father. "You know that you can only marry a Jewish girl."

Julius was furious, devastated, but resolved. They were in love. Klara was heartbroken, shattered but not shocked. Her parents were not surprised, and perhaps a bit relieved. Anti-Semitism had not disappeared with the Paris Peace Treaties.

Over the following weeks, multitudes of angry discussions ensued, two households torn apart. The couple agonized, schemed, fretted over a solution to their dilemma. Parent-child communications were severed.

One evening, exhausted, full of anger and self-pity, Klara sat on the edge of her bed, trying to take solace in the old, yellowing photo of her "real parents" within her gold ankle locket as she had done hundreds of times before--for as long as she could remember. No one actually had ever told her or any of the children at the nunnery what happened to their parents.

Klara noticed for the first time a corner of the photo peeling away. There appeared to be an object sealed just below it. Klara peeled back the photo, and below was a small piece of folded parchment. She carefully removed and unfolded the old but intact piece of graying paper and read the message within (in German): "Your name is Sadie Levine. The world will scorn this plague on humanity. Know always that you are Jewish, we love you dearly, and hope you will remember us in your heart forever. Sh'ma Yisrael. Love, Mother and Father."

Sadie and Julius Bloom were pronounced husband and wife several weeks later. Susan was born one year later.

# War Story

Susan Bloom was always very focused. She knew what she wanted. She knew that she would finish up at the two-year community college in New Bedford and then complete her education in Boston. She was great at math and was headed toward a career as a certified public accountant. Her plan was simple. Work hard, get good grades, earn her degree. Susan worked diligently in her parents' clothing manufacturing business most days and went to school at night.

Julius and Sadie were hardworking, toiling at Bloom's Apparel, from morning to dusk. They had little time for social events or special occasions. Their daughter and their business were their life. Yes, they did celebrate Passover, Rosh Hashanah, and Yom Kippur, but they rarely went to temple. Knowing that their personal, family, and cultural histories were riddled with stories of Euro-Asian pogroms and Holocaust atrocities, they both felt that if God existed, He sure kept himself well hidden.

At first, Susan's father or mother would pick her up at night from junior college, or she'd take the bus home. During her second year, Susan noticed that a classmate and friend, Dawn, would get a ride from her boyfriend, Eddy. Dawn was an economics major as well.

Eddy was polite, good-looking in an ethnic type of way, and kind. He owned Eddy's Luncheonette downtown. He would wait for Dawn in the library, and soon offered to take Susan home as well. Susan got to know both Dawn and Eddy in a superficial but friendly way. The threesome occasionally went for a drink or a cup of coffee. Small talk.

Around midterm of their second year, Dawn told both Eddy and Susan that she was moving. Her father was being transferred to the Naval Station, Norfolk, Virginia.

One month later, Susan "happened" to run into Eddy when she decided to stop for a cup of coffee at the luncheonette near closing time. He offered her a ride home that night and every night thereafter.

Eddy loved to read, and he would consume book after book in the library, waiting for Susan to get out of class.

He liked how smart, independent, and, of course, how attractive she was, with jet-black hair wavy to her shoulders, brilliant blue eyes, and an athletic figure. Susan liked how Eddy was down-to-earth, inquisitive, honest, kind, and a consistently nice guy. Their attraction for one another grew steadily.

Susan completed her education as a commuter student, traveling back and forth to Boston for two years. After graduation, as planned, she started her own one-woman CPA firm. Like Eddy, Susan had a strong work ethic, and each of them established their own financial security.

It was a brief courtship. Eddy was introduced to Susan's family with its Jewish heritage. He was impressed by the symbolism, the loyalties, the pride and traditions that were the bedrock of Susan's family.

Susan was initiated into the cultural aspects of Eddy's close-knit Armenian family. She was struck by the quiet with which Armenians remembered their holocaust even as Jews lived by the hue and cry of "Never Again!"

They took dancing lessons at Arthur Murray's Dance School and planned to be married on an autumn day under a tent in the Bloom's back yard.

After an evening of discussing the wedding plans at the home of Eddy's parents, Aram and Sonia Moravian, Aram walked over to Eddy on his way out the door. He handed his son a white piece of paper folded in half. "To be opened when you leave," Aram said with a smile, patting Eddy on the shoulder.

Eddy stuck the note in his pocket, took Susan's hand, said good-bye, closed the door, and walked Susan to the car. In the driveway, before putting the car into gear, Eddy took out the piece of paper from his pocket, unfolded it, and leaned over so Susan could read the message with him.

I WOULD APPRECIATE YOUR INVITING MR. AND MRS. STEIN TO THE WEDDING. THANK YOU.

Eddy and Susan turned to each other with quizzical looks. After a moment, unable to decipher the puzzling request, they drove off toward home.

* * *

Eddy and Susan were married on a beautiful afternoon in early September. With all the fun and festivities, the air got a bit stuffy inside the reception tent. Eddy decided to take a break and walked outside to get some fresh air. He could still hear the echoing sounds of his father's Middle Eastern band playing as he approached the balding, bull-dog of a figure leaning against the fence surrounding the property.

"Beautiful autumn day," said Eddy.

"The best," replied Moishie. He relit his cigar, a soggy stub, almost burning his nose.

Eddy still could not quite figure out how Moishie and his father were connected, so he just came right out and asked.

Moishie's eyebrows rose, and his brow furrowed.

"You're kidding, right?" Moishie stared at Eddy, his expression incredulous.

"No, no. I'm not kidding," said Eddy. He cocked his head a bit to the side. Neither Aram, Eddy's father, nor Moishie had ever mentioned the other to Eddy as best as he could remember.

Moishie took a long drag on his Cuban cigar, blew out the smoke into the light breeze, and sighed.

"Well, it's about time you heard the story."

"What story? About you and my dad? My quiet father?" The fact that those two knew each other, let alone had a story to tell, the story, confused Eddy. Events of his father's past that he didn't know about?

Moishie's eyes glistened as he began the story.

"Your dad is not only quiet, but brave, strong, kind, relentless, loyal, and courageous."

***

Moses Stein from Boston and Aram Moravian from Watertown were drafted into the same unit in the army during World War II and saw action in the Pacific theater. The two bunk mates were part of a "clean up" duty that arrived on the island one week following the Battle of Okinawa. That Pacific battle was won by the Allies but the casualties were enormous. American casualties were 49,000, including 12,500 killed; 110,000 Japanese soldiers lost their lives, and somewhere between 50,000 and 150,000 Japanese citizens died.

When the pontoon boats from the ships arrived on the shoreline, stacks of bodies piled eight feet high by twenty feet wide by 300 hundred feet lined the beachhead. The American soldiers' reactions to the gruesome scene led to a gloomy aura that surrounded the US Army barracks on the east side of the island. No one actually knew whether all of the enemy had been rooted out. On occasion, some stragglers could be found in various caves in the mountains. How many resistance fighters were still out there, nobody knew. Because of this the enlisted men were constantly on edge.

Most of the guys at the camp made a few good friends and many acquaintances, and the usual cliques would form among the soldiers. Though he was a quiet fellow who kept to himself, everyone at the camp knew Private First-Class Aram Moravian. No one called him by his given name; all the men knew him as "Marv." Marv was short for Marvelous.

The big events of the week were the fights. All weight classes except featherweight were included. Aram was the star of the camp.

Marvelous Moravian, a heavyweight, was undefeated. Moravian was lanky, had dark black curly hair, and a big bushy mustache that curled up in a way that made it look like he was always smiling. He was pure muscle, not an ounce of fat, and he was Herculean strong.

Every time he won a fight—and he won every time he was in the ring—he would help his opponent off the mat, walk to his corner, raise his arm, say thank you to the crowd, and go quietly off to the showers and then to his bunk. Never any fanfare.

His good buddy, Moishie, controlled most of the action for Marv's fights. Some of the guys won a good bit of change on the fights, but they lost their week's pay more often than not. Moishie always made out quite nicely, thank you.

On the night of concern, Aram had just won another fight and was sitting, freshly showered, on his bunk, looking a little down in the mouth. Moishie was on his bunk, counting the huge wad of dollar bills he had just "struggled" to win.

"Hey Moishie, I was wondering whether you would do me a big favor?" asked Aram.

Moishie stuffed the wad of bills into the left breast pocket of his shirt.

"Sure, anything you want, Marv."

It was the last day of Aram's tour of duty.

"Listen, Moishie, you know it's my last night here. I'm scheduled to ship out in the morning, back home to the states. Somehow, I pulled guard duty on my last night. I was hoping to have a few beers with the guys, get my stuff ready, and take off at zero-five-hundred tomorrow. Do you think you could take my guard duty for tonight?"

Moishie had a good heart. Aram had made him a rich Corporal.

"Sure, buddy. Have a beer on me. I got a few more weeks myself. If you're not asleep, I may have a frosty with you when I get back."

A little after midnight, Aram thought, Moishie should be back by now. A feeling deep in his gut told him that something wasn't right. He rose from his cot, put on his shirt and buttoned it enough to keep it closed, laced up his boots, and walked to the perimeter wall.

Moishie had been walking the wall surrounding the barracks for four hours. His shift was over. As he reached into his pocket for a cigarette that he would light when he came down off the wall, he heard an almost imperceptible click. At the same moment, he felt a sudden intense pain in his back. An arm caught his neck in a vise. He glimpsed a shiny object crash into his left chest. He jabbed into his assailant's ribs with his left elbow, heard a crack, and bit down on the arm around him as hard as he could. A scream pierced the quiet night air as Moishie ripped a piece of flesh from the bone, but not before a searing pain scalded down his upper right arm. He grabbed the knife, swung around, and stabbed into the dark. His knife met some resistance, then sunk in, and with his last ounce of strength, Moishie pulled down with all his might. A thump on the ground revealed a bloodied Japanese soldier, gutted, with entrails spilling from within. Adrenaline coursing through him, Moishie scrambled over the wall, landing ten feet down on his left ankle, which splintered on impact.

Using hands and knees, Moishie crawled until, sapped of strength, he collapsed under a grove of tall palm trees. He heard gunshots from all directions. The enemy was getting closer. He was exhausted. Corporal Stein was drifting into unconsciousness when he thought he heard a rustling noise to his left. He felt something squeeze his left elbow.

"Hey, Moishie, it's Aram," whispered a voice.

Moishie thought he was imagining his friend, but he mumbled,

"Marv, you've got to get out of here. They're coming to kill us. There's no way out."

Aram put his right index finger up to his lips.

For several seconds he looked around in every direction. Then he took a closer look at his friend's wounds. Moishie's left ankle was shattered, and his foot dangled unnaturally by several thin tendons. His right arm was hemorrhaging from a deep gash in his upper deltoid.

Aram took his government-issued shirt and tied it around Moishie's ankle. He took one bootlace and wrapped it around the shirt. He took the other bootlace and tied it around his buddy's upper right arm. Though the bleeding stopped, Moishie's moans grew louder. Aram took his T-shirt and stuffed it in his friend's mouth. He took his heavy boots and flung them, one at a time, as far as he could, one to the right and one to the left. Each made a crashing noise in the bushes beyond as it landed. He then picked up Moishie, slung him over his shoulder, and shimmied up the tallest tree in sight. No branches, nothing to hang on to, propelled upward by sheer strength alone. At the top, hidden by the gigantic fronds, was one secure palm branch that might have a chance of supporting their combined weight. Aram hung on to that branch with one arm while he held his friend with the other.

***

"And we stayed up there all night," said Moishie. "One hundred and ten degrees. Me, passed out. Six fucking hours. Then, when the coast was clear, he climbed down and dragged my ass back to base. They flew me to Australia, to a major military hospital. They somehow put my ankle back together. They saved my arm. And shipped me back home. The doctors said that if I didn't have that wad of money in my shirt pocket, that Japanese stiletto would have gone clear through to my heart. I would've been a goner."

Eddy's mouth was agape as Moishie concluded his story and then added softly,

"We haven't seen each other for 30 years. Until today."

# Cote d'Ivoire

Molly was at the top of her high school class academically. She won the first prize in the science fair every year. As a senior, she received her acceptance letter to the six-year medical program at Harvard. She kept her head down and her nose clean. She was a true Goody-Two-Shoes.

Not that she wasn't adventurous. Her parents became unsettled when they all met with the high school academic adviser to discuss her future. They were already so proud that she was going to medical school. However, Molly announced at that meeting that on her own, she had arranged and had been awarded a grant, specifically designed for young women scientists, from the Gilbert and Zelda Bates Institute.

She was to spend three months in Africa, to learn about prevention and eradication of endemic diseases. Ivory Coast to be exact. She would be working in a clinic there, room and board provided. She'd also be giving swimming lessons to indigent children.

* * *

As Molly walked off the plane, the hot air hit her like the sigh from a fire-breathing dragon. It had been a long flight from John F. Kennedy International in New York to Abidjan, Cote d'Ivoire on the west coast of Africa. High school graduation, two weeks ago, already seemed like an event of the distant past. She was unsure what to expect despite the internet searches she had done.

"I can't wait," Molly said with a smile when the U.S. program director told her she'd been assigned to Cote d'Ivoire for three months.

She learned that Côte d'Ivoire (labeled as the Ivory Coast on American atlases) is a North African country of 25,000,000 people. The French colony gained its independence in 1960. This Sub-Saharan country contributed over 40% of the world's cocoa harvest.

Abidjan was the largest city, the economic center, and it sat on the eastern seacoast looking out to the Gulf of Guinea. Most Ivorians were cocoa farmers or processors, the backbone of a struggling economy. It was a poor country, with about 40% of the populace living below the poverty line. Approximately 60% earned less than $3.20 per day.

She felt strangled by the oppressive heat and near-100% humidity as she walked across the tarmac toward the gray steel-and-glass welcome center. Approaching Customs, Baggage, and Security, she saw a tall, skinny man, in his forties wearing a loosely fitting flowered short-sleeve shirt, black khakis, and black woven sandals. He carried a small white cardboard sign printed in black Magic Marker that read 'MS. MORAVIAN.' When Molly walked up to him, he gave her a wide, toothy grin and said,

"Bonjour, mademoiselle. Je m'appelle Jacques."

"Bonjour, monsieur. I am Molly."

"S'il vous plait," said Jacques as he took her backpack with his left hand and began walking while signaling with his right hand the way one does when they want you to follow them for a short distance.

"Allons-y."

The place was a madhouse, a crowd consisting of new arrivals, friends and relatives, taxi drivers, policemen, tee-shirt and beaded necklace vendors. Molly was able to point out her checked baggage consisting of two black duffels on one of three luggage trolleys. Jacques removed them, amidst a sea of grabbing hands, checked the tags, helped Molly meander her way through the bag check and Customs, and out the glass exit doors into the furnace-like heat again.

Molly caught a whiff of salty ocean air, smog, and a bit of her own perspiration. They walked down a flagstone walkway for about 100 feet to the curb, where cars of all makes and models, mostly old, were lined up waiting. Her escort stopped at a muted green Land Rover, put Molly's bags in the car, and came around to the passenger side to open the back door. Molly cautiously stuck her head in, immediately felt cooler air, and at the same time heard someone with a French accent yell from the front seat,

"Thank you, Jacques."

On the heels of getting in, she heard the same deep, welcoming voice say, "Bonjour. You must be Miss Molly. I am Dr. Pierre Rodin. Welcome to Cote d'Ivoire."

Dr. Pierre Rodin is handsome was the first thought that came into Molly's head. He threw his right arm over the driver's seat and twisted around to greet her. He had skin the color of nutmeg, short brown hair, tortoiseshell glasses, straight pearly white teeth, an irresistible mouth, with a soothing baritone voice.

Molly said, "Hello, how do you do?"

Dr. Rodin's eyebrows peaked while his mouth and lips formed a grin that curled up in an intoxicating fashion. As the car sped away from the airport on a two-lane road, Molly took in the azure ocean on the right. They negotiated a roundabout and merged into the traffic of the inner city. The rich smell of spices, the colorful fabrics, and people walking along a road lined with palm trees quickly gave way to a picture of a thriving city of low-rise buildings. Looming above the homes were several high-rises, apartment buildings, business centers, an enormous soccer stadium, hotel towers, and a number of long, beautiful bridges spanning various inlets and waterways within the city limits.

"All this construction occurred in the last ten to twenty years as Cote d'Ivoire emerged from civil war in about 2000," explained Dr. Rodin as they drove. "What you see now is the government's attempt to modernize, including several international beachside resorts and spas." He briefly explained some history of the country and some issues regarding healthcare.

"This is still a very poor country. Poverty leads to poor healthcare. Not only is the medical care inadequate in the countryside and interior of the country, but even in our few major cities the healthcare systems are sorely lacking. We are going to stop at the clinic just outside the city. You will meet the staff, and then we will drive to my home to get you settled. You have had a long flight."

They finally stopped at a one-story yellow brick building with a red-tiled roof and a 20-foot-porch that wrapped around the front. Six plastic chairs were strewn about in a haphazard fashion across the lawn. A small wooden sign painted red with yellow lettering above the main entrance read LE CENTRE MEDICAL, DISTRICT DE LAGUNES/ABIDJAN.

It was noontime. Dr. Rodin tooted the horn as he stopped the car. They got out and walked toward the entrance. Three women and two men came through the door and unfolded a paper banner that read, "Welcome Miss Molly." They all smiled and shook Molly's hand.

"This is Sita, Aya, and Madeline," said the doctor as the women greeted Molly.

The men, Koffi and Yaya, introduced themselves as well. After glasses of ginger beer were passed around, they raised their glasses. "Sainté!" everyone shouted before downing their beverages. The staff then returned to work as the doctor showed Molly briefly around the clinic.

Then Molly and Dr. Rodin drove for a short while down a long gravel road to the outskirts of the city,. They stopped at a white stucco house with burnt orange shutters and a filigreed black iron gate. Molly admired the white stone wall surrounding the house with magenta bougainvillea cascading down all sides. A small, balding, older man appeared from the house. He opened the gate and allowed the car to pull into the property. A grassy lawn within the confines of the wall encircled the home. A 30-meter lap pool fit into the southwest corner of the yard. On top of the house sat a huge gray metal cistern.

Pierre Rodin officially introduced Molly to Jacques who had helped her out at the airport, and to Felix, who had opened the iron gate to the property. They entered the house, Molly was given a brief tour of Dr. Rodin's home, finally showing his guest to her bedroom.

Molly thanked her host, excused herself, and, exhausted, got into bed and slept clear through the night.

Dr. Pierre Rodin sat in his Ruthann wing chair by the bay window in his study, ignoring the medical journal in his lap. As he stared at the full moon, he raised his wine glass to welcome his new mentee. She would fill a void.

# Worlds Apart

At dawn, the day promised to be incredibly hot and humid. Due to the ocean breezes coming from the Atlantic, Abidjan was on average 10 degrees cooler than the interior of the country. But it was still blazing hot.

Each of the six rooms of the clinic contained a large ceiling fan. On the few days when there were no problems with the electricity, stand-alone fans were used as well, particularly in the laboratory and the petite chirurgie room for small surgical procedures.

Molly, in her white smock, stood hunched over a little girl, waiting for the thermometer to ripen. In the month since she had started in the medical clinic, Molly was shown how to register each patient—children in the morning and adults in the afternoon—take their temperature, blood pressure and pulse, and have them sit or lie down in a curtain-bound space depending on their complaint. The mothers were always worried; the children were invariably shy but polite as they remained close to their mother's side.

The three women nurses who also wore clean white smocks, scurried around administering medicine, giving injections and vaccinations, and dressing minor wounds. A constant backbeat of chatter in French could be heard above the frequent cries, shouts, moans, and groans. The two male nurses in their white waist-length jackets worked mostly in the lab drawing and processing blood work.

They sometimes assisted in surgical procedures, took X-rays, and did the heavy lifting when needed. Dr. Pierre Rodin walked from stall to stall taking histories, doing physical exams, reading X-rays, setting broken bones, and holding hands—sometimes children's, mothers', and sometimes those of staff members. Molly observed the doctor as he interacted with the patients.

Dr. Rodin approached each patient serenely, listened to their complaints and talked with them in a relaxed and easy manner. He examined them with his soft, steady hands, and explained to them with a kind and caring demeanor what the problem might be and what would be required. He worked from early in the morning to dusk, stopping for perhaps a cup of tea and maybe a Parisian sandwich of ham and cheese on a buttered baguette. All the while, he would talk to Molly about medicine.

The most common diseases he treated were malaria, tuberculosis, and HIV/AIDS, the latter being the leading cause of death in the country. He might see other infections such as yellow fever and dengue fever, parasitic infections including African trypanosomiasis, onchocerciasis, leishmaniasis, schistosomiasis; and viruses such as Ebola and bacterial infections including typhoid, typhus, and others. He told Molly that she would rarely see any of the latter illnesses in the U.S.

From the readings Dr. Rodin gave her in the first weeks after her arrival, Molly learned the two worlds of medicine and diseases were eons apart. In the US, the leading causes of death were heart disease and cancer, but in Cote d'Ivoire malaria, HIV/AIDS, neonatal disorders, lower respiratory infections and diarrheal diseases topped the list.

Each day at sundown, the clinic would close, the doctor and student would drive home, have a home-cooked meal, and talk throughout the evening. Dr. Rodin would share his thoughts about the art of medicine, about being true to oneself, and mindfulness. He would explain that mindfulness was an attempt to de-stress, think more clearly, and pay attention to one's inner and outer experiences. Molly could listen to him all night.

One evening as they both sipped a bit of cognac, Molly paid special attention when Pierre shared some of his background.

"I was born in this country. My father owned a number of local cocoa plantations, and my mother was relocated to Côte d'Ivoire by the Parisian chocolate company that she worked for. I worked hard in school, moved to France and received my medical education at the Université de Paris. I married a medical school classmate, from Saint-Denis. We practiced and lived in Paris for a short while. I wanted to give back to my parents and to my country, so we moved back to Cote d'Ivoire. Within a year of returning here, my young wife was diagnosed with stage four breast cancer and died in less than six months."

His silence felt like a shroud. After a few moments Molly spoke up. "I am so sorry," said Molly. "I don't know how you moved on from there."

Dr. Rodin paused for a long while before saying softly,

"I love my work, I love my patients, and I love my country." He paused again. "I am trying to make a difference."

He looked at her with his large brown eyes, and with a soothing smile, said, "So, have you found the medicine interesting so far?"

Molly thought about the unusual cases, the strength of these people to endure many of the diseases that had been eradicated in the US for decades.

"Excuse me, I don't mean to be rude, but why haven't we seen one case of cancer since I have been here? While I am glad for your patients that we haven't, we've seen no adults with any cancer diagnoses, and no child with lymphoma or leukemia. Does that seem odd to you? Or maybe I just don't know what I am talking about."

"Non, ma chere that is a very brilliant question," Dr. Rodin raised his eyebrows and cocked his head to the left, as a thin smile spread across his sensitive, intelligent face. "We have been asking ourselves this for decades. No one knows the answer. The water? The air? Inherent genetic resistance? Maybe you will be the one to solve this one day."

Pierre moved his head closer to Molly's. He placed a warm hand on her left knee. Molly's heart skipped a beat. She felt warm all over, and it wasn't from the cognac.

"And with that, I bid you bonne soiree," said Pierre. "We will talk about many more great things tomorrow."

* * *

Molly glided through the water with ease. As her endorphins kicked in, she grinned with exhilaration every time she did her laps. She couldn't stop thinking of Pierre, who was swimming laps in the other lane.

As they did each morning at the least hot and sticky time of the day, Molly and Dr. Rodin rose early, donned their swim suits, and dove into the lap pool in the corner of the compound behind the protective white stone wall. They'd swim their laps together, then dry off poolside. Pierre couldn't help but notice his beautiful and strong student, her long, dark hair gleaming in the sun. Molly saw her tall and lean mentor in his Speedo swimsuit, his smooth skin still damp from the swim.

They would proceed to the house, get dressed, eat breakfast, and drive to the clinic. Before leaving for work, Molly would often send off a quick email to her parents, always signing it with her initials, M.O.M. She saved an evening once a week to send an email to her best friend, Kitty. By way of reciprocal letters over the years there emerged a trust in each other, a sharing of private thoughts and experiences regardless of the miles that separated them..

Two mornings a week, Dr. Rodin practiced at a rural clinic in the interior of the country an hour northwest of Abidjan. He would drop Molly at the public beach on the bayside, where she would teach swimming to children, doing the best she could to communicate with them in her rudimentary French.

She taught the basics to those who were just getting used to the salt water and waves. To others, who had advanced nicely over the past several weeks, she taught the crawl, breaststroke, butterfly, side stroke, and backstroke. She was patient, kind, persistent, and fun-loving. She always saved the last fifteen minutes for "free swim/playtime." As time went on, she accrued more students. The children would crowd around her, some so excited that they did not want to run into the waiting arms of their mothers who came to pick them up at lunchtime.

Dr. Pierre Rodin and his staff spent those two mornings in the interior triaging families in the district according to the most urgent cases, educating parents and teaching classes on sex education, AIDS/HIV, and basic hygiene and sanitation. They developed group vaccination schedules and set up special hours for obstetrics, gynecology, and, of course, the diarrhea clinic. Dr. Rodin oversaw pharmacy supplies, distribution, methods of refills, and strategies to ensure that medication instructions were adhered to. Although there was always the issue of patient distrust to deal with, most farmers and their families were compliant, thankful for the doctor's professional, caring ways.

As he worked, Molly's question about cancer was a recurring enigma that scratched at his mind. He and his colleagues were usually too busy stamping out daily maladies like malaria, HIV, cholera, and neonatal complications to delve into a fact-finding mission. And why should they? Cancer was number 50 on his country's list of most common causes of death. Nonetheless, he couldn't help admire Molly's keen mind, recognizing her as one of a new generation of world travelers and solution seekers searching for answers to the unknown.

# Alone on the Farm

For the past several weekends, Dr. Rodin had begun taking Molly with him to visit his parents and family in the interior of the country. They would start out in the morning heading due north, passing the thousands of jungle farmland plantations on the way. Nothing but cocoa farms filled the view on the left, right, and in front of them.

They were greeted with smiles, hugs, and food upon their arrival at the family farm. They would sit down for the noon meal to enjoy attiéké (fermented cassava), garba (attiéké and fish), chicken, tubers, and of course chocolate for dessert. His parents' four-room house was made of cinder blocks, with a terra-cotta floor and a tin roof. A grassy front yard was filled with chickens clucking about and an outhouse could be found down a short trail. The property opened up to thousands of cocoa trees intermingled with an assortment of colorful banana, plantain, mango trees—and pineapple plants. The family would usually spend the day talking and walking, or occasionally taking a ride out to Taabo Lake, formed by the damming of the Bandana River.

One Saturday, Molly and the doctor stopped about halfway to the Rodin farm to visit the large cocoa plantation owned by Pierre's friend Adam Bekoin. After exchanging warm greetings, Adam offered to give them a tour of his working cocoa farm.

Adam explained the long process of cultivation, from the ten years' time it takes the Theobroma cacao (food of the gods) tree to mature until the beans are dried to perfection and placed in burlap bags to be delivered around the world. Molly saw hundreds of workers covered in cocoa dust, hands sticky from cocoa butter, working in air laden with cocoa fragrance. Some even waded into the bags to stuff them for export.

During the tour, Adam talked of his country's dark history. The farming of cocoa in Ivory Coast reaped a bittersweet harvest.

Exploitation and low wages led to severe poverty, poor health care, inadequate education, and poor housing.

Molly was told that efforts had been made in recent years to reverse the endemic problems. Women farmers, who did 70% of the work on the farms, established a fair-trade cooperative, CAYAT, in 2010. CAYAT was a coffee and cocoa farming cooperative based near the large towns in the south of Côte d'Ivoire. Companies had to agree to buy and sell chocolate on fair-trade terms.

Economic programs were set up to improve the financial equation in cocoa farming communities. Women empowerment led to protecting children's rights. Goals were set to improve the social, educational, and economic status of the working farmers and their families. Poverty was an ongoing issue but with heightened awareness and more fair-trade associations forming, the deep-seated problem was beginning to be addressed.

"Of course, as you have seen, despite these efforts, our people still live in abject poverty," Pierre concluded.

"It certainly will make me think twice the next time I eat a chocolate candy bar," Molly said. "How could something as wonderful and delicious as a chocolate candy bar have its roots in such gruesome, unfair circumstances?"

At the end of the tour, Pierre and Molly said their goodbyes and resumed their drive to Pierre's parents' farm. Molly and Pierre talked about how practically everyone in Cote' d'Ivoire—man, woman, and child—worked in the cocoa industry and were in constant contact with cocoa pods, cocoa beans, and cocoa powder.

That piece of chocolate wrapped in colorful foil left on your pillow in the hotel bedroom? How did it get there? No, not who brought it there, but how was it made? thought Molly following the tour of Adam's plantation.

She couldn't get chocolate off her mind, but neither could she stop thinking about Dr. Rodin. Molly loved talking with Pierre; she could talk to him all day and into the night … and she did. On car rides and at home they discussed the cultural, economic, social, health, and political aspects of the all-encompassing $5 billion per year enterprise of King Chocolate. They'd review medical lore and history, diagnosing, treating, and preventing some of the oldest and most dreaded conditions that had plagued this population for centuries. Often, however the pair would revert back to the question that most intrigued this inquisitive American medical student: What prevented the people of this country from developing cancer? This answer was like a cocoa bean, enveloped in a shell, wrapped in fibrous tissue, and protected within a pod.

* * *

As they drove up to the farm, there was not the usual welcome from the staff. Rodin suddenly remembered that this was the weekend of the annual Cocoa Festival. The entire village would have left to attend. The family had apparently gone to Yamoussoukro for the festival. It was a weekend-long affair offering music, dancing, cooking, eating, and family games. There were also speeches and some politics, of course, wrapped in a sea of colorful dresses, garish headpieces, laughter, and fun.

Molly and Pierre found themselves alone on the farm.

"Did you know that the first mechanized chocolate factory was built in Switzerland in the 1819?" Molly asked with a beguiling smile. "I researched this. The world has a love affair with chocolate but did you know who the most amorous consumers of chocolate are?"

Pierre cocked an eyebrow in a curious manner as he placed food and utensils into a picnic basket.

"Switzerland, Austria, Germany, Iceland, Great Britain, Sweden, Estonia, Norway, Poland, Belgium, Finland, and the Netherlands, in that order, consume the most chocolate. I was surprised to find that the United States is not even close to making this list."

"Well, I have done some research of my own," Pierre answered. "Let me tell you about it when we sit."

They carried some sliced ham, a fresh baguette, cheese, wine, and two oranges to a wooden, screened gazebo beside a small stream. They sat down close to one another on a multicolored handwoven blanket. Pierre moved close, his arm touching Molly's. She did not move away.

"I will complete the story of the making of chocolate," he said in a low voice. "You see, once the burlap bags of cocoa beans are shipped from Cote d'Ivoire, they arrive at the chocolate producers: Cadbury, Nestlé, Chocolat Frey AG. Some of the quality variables include the type and size of beans, the specific hybrid, what farms they were grown on, and what insects and molds they have been exposed to. After the inspection stage, the beans are washed and then roasted for 10 to 40 minutes to separate the hard shell from the bean kernel. The cracked bean kernels are called cocoa nibs. The nibs contain about 50% cocoa butter (which is pure fat), and 50% cocoa powder.

Molly chewed as she eyed Pierre, unable to look away even as crumbs spilled onto her lap.

"The nibs are then milled in great grinders called melangeurs and crushed at high speed," he continued. "The heat causes the powder to liquefy with the cocoa butter. The cocoa butter coats the pearl-shaped particles. The smaller the particles, the smoother the chocolate. Cocoa butter is responsible for the flavor, the silky textures, and the cooling effect on your tongue.

"The mixture is then placed through conching machines that roll and paddle the chocolate, constantly kneading it for hours or days, getting rid of the bitterness, honing the flavor, giving it that melt in your mouth quality. The mélange is massaged, tempered, aerated and the chocolate mass is then poured into molds, cooled, and wrapped."

"Fini," said Pierre with a warm smile, looking straight into Molly's eyes. It was the end of August; the weather was a little cooler, and a brief drizzle had tapered off. The sky was clear, and the Rodin property was quiet as the sun began to set. Molly and Pierre sat under the open sky past dusk, listening to the crickets chirp and finishing their after-dinner glasses of wine.

Placing his glass aside, Dr. Rodin rose and extended his hand. "Let's take a walk." He guided Molly to her feet.

Molly stood close to him. She had been dreaming about this moment for months. They walked in silence for a time, hand in hand, down a moonlit path.

"You know. Molly," Pierre said finally, "it's been such a pleasure to be with you these last three months. You've awakened thoughts and feelings in me that I have not had in quite some time."

Warm feelings stirred in Molly, the same ones that she had been having for weeks. "Thanks for being so good to me," she whispered. "I'll be sad to leave next week."

He turned to her, took her gently in his arms, and kissed her. Molly closed her eyes and pulled him closer. She wanted that moment to never end. Pierre gently guided her back to the house. Molly was overcome by her desires. She trusted Pierre. She felt safe in his arms. Her passion for him was overwhelming.

Pierre led Molly to the bedroom.

***

Does a sound exist if there is no one there to hear it? Maybe only the chickens heard the moans and sighs coming from the Rodin ancestral home that August evening. Pierre and Molly woke to the sounds of bugs and birds. She was still in his arms and wanted to stay there forever. Several hours passed, amid more sounds of pleasure.

"When the student is ready..." Pierre mused.

"...the teacher will appear." Molly finished the sentence for him.

"You came here a young girl looking for a medical protégé," Pierre said, "and you will leave us as a woman at the beginning of a wonderful career in medicine."

"You made it possible," Molly said, lifting her head for yet another kiss.

Dr. Pierre Rodin finally rose from their bed and made them each a cup of espresso. As the morning heat surged he drove them slowly down the jungle hills toward Abidjan.

Molly's head was swimming. Over the next several days, she had to pack, say good-bye to friends, and prepare for her early-morning flight home. She would start her six-year medical program the following week.

# At Home Test

The foliage of Boston in autumn was changing as Molly began her undergraduate/medical school program at Harvard University. The memory of her time in Africa was already beginning to fade, but her heart and mind often drifted toward Dr. Pierre Rodin.

While she handled the schoolwork easily, she did not feel like herself, physically or emotionally. As the semester progressed, she felt bloated, nauseated (especially in the morning), her breasts seemed bigger, and strangely, her nipples appeared darker.

"I feel like a cow," cried Molly on the phone to her best friend Kitty. "I'm gaining weight by the day, and I feel like crying at the drop of a hat. And, oh yeah, I missed my period."

Kitty went to the pharmacy with Molly to purchase a pregnancy test.

"God damn it," yelled Molly with tears in her eyes as she and her friend read the positive pregnancy test. Kitty put her arm around her friend's shoulder as they sat down together on the den couch, Molly slumping over, crying into the palms of her hands.

"Should I call Pierre?" she asked.

Kitty, practical as ever, pooh-poohed the idea.

"For what? You're worried about what having a baby will do to your career, do you really think he will chuck it all and come over here to be a proud papa with a woman he barely knew?"

Molly was silent. She knew that having a baby could jeopardize, if not derail, her future.

"I'm falling behind in my schoolwork and I've been skipping classes," Molly wailed. "My chemistry teacher pulled me aside and asked me how I was doing, and I said fine, but I thought that I was going to throw up on her any minute. This pregnancy is messing me up already and it's barely started."

Kitty gave her a long look. Molly knew her options were limited. She did not weigh her options for very long. Kitty helped her to make an appointment for an in-clinic abortion at Planned Parenthood.

Her Planned Parenthood appointment was in two weeks. Molly's life had turned from one of excited optimism, to one of overwhelming despair.

"I'm glad I have your friendship and support, Kitty," she said. "I could never tell my parents. And thanks for offering to go with me to the clinic."

Should I call Pierre? thought Molly again, as she walked home from the library one night. Tears rolled down her cheeks. She vomited on the sidewalk. She balanced herself against a nearby telephone pole.

What would he say? What would he think? He can't come to comfort me. Why should I burden him with my problem?

Molly stood up straight. She tried to catch her breath. I shouldn't and I won't, she sniffled. What good could come of it now?

She had never felt so alone. Molly dragged herself home as an intense wave of nausea hit. She opened the door to the apartment, quickly threw her backpack on the kitchen chair, and ran to the bathroom just in time to vomit.

"Oh, my God," she screamed, and collapsed on the bed in a torrent of tears amidst the loneliness, the anger, the self-doubt, and the myriad of unresolved feelings.

***

Molly woke in the middle of the night with abdominal cramps like she had never had before. She went to the bathroom and sat on the toilet but the unbearable cramps continued. Suddenly, she had a large amount of bloody vaginal discharge. She noticed several blood clots. Her cramps lasted several more hours, as she remained crying in the bathroom until she couldn't cry anymore.

Later that night, exhausted, Molly sat with her friend.

"Kitty, thanks for coming over. I feel so bad. You're the only one I could call. You realize, of course, that I'm not going to need that freaking clinic visit."

"I know, Molly, I know. But we're together forever," Kitty said, holding her weeping friend close.

"What should I tell Pierre?" Molly asked. "I should have told him that I was carrying his child."

"Why?' Kitty asked, ever the pragmatic. "You're the Harvard doc-to-be, but even I know, baby, that sometimes the truth just isn't enough. Keep it to yourself and move on."

They cried together for a long time and then Molly went to bed and slept for 12 hours. Kitty cancelled Molly's Planned Parenthood appointment.

# Chemistry Between Them

Walking across the M.I.T. campus, Aaron Katz put his chin down, buttoned up his coat, and shoved his hands in his pockets, as he felt the brisk late autumn wind push against him.

"Hey Aaron," yelled Jerry, one of Aaron's Ultimate Frisbee teammates, from across the quad.

Aaron waved and thought, "I'll be happy to get into Building 24, to the warmth of my next class. Especially in that seat right behind *her.*"

Aaron grew up in a small two-bedroom ranch, right next to the community college in New Bedford, where his mother taught biology and his father taught chemistry. As a boy, Aaron quickly became bored with the multiple chemistry sets and build-your -own rocket kits he was given. He mastered every game, puzzle, and Rubrik's cube with which he was challenged.

As a child, the ambiance was calm and quiet in his house, particularly after his younger brother, Jack, died in a car accident in which the four of them had been involved. That accident was rarely discussed.

In grade school, he was told to sit in the corner most days of the week for disrupting the class. He was bored and restless, but very smart and inquisitive.

"Does your family have any chairs at home?" his grade school teacher would ask, or sometimes simply pronounce,

"If I were your parents, I would kill myself."

But Aaron remained at the top of his class scholastically. His parents simply thought he had "ants in his pants," or *schpilkes.* In junior high school, the teachers' annoyance with him continued. One advanced-math teacher, when giving the final exam of the year, made Aaron sit right in front of his desk so he wouldn't "cheat." When Aaron handed in his exam half way through the time allotted and received a grade of 100% (110% with extra credit), his teacher took him by the shirt collar and led him into the coat closet.

"You could not possibly have gotten 110% on that test without cheating," the teacher screamed.

In high school at Taylor Academy, a private boys' school about twenty minutes from New Bedford, Aaron continued to excel in the classroom as well as on the playing field. Once, while participating in a soccer tournament, when called a *kike* by an opposing player during a match, he hauled off and punched his opponent in the face, invoking his disqualification and suspension from school.

***

"You've got it, you've got it," a friend at MIT kept teasing him. Aaron Katz had no idea what he meant. His friend finally explained that he himself had ADHD and thought Aaron did as well.

"Takes one to know one," his friend explained.

As soon as he was placed on Ritalin, the mainstay treatment for ADHD, he focused better, performed better in the classroom and concentrated like never before. He was not as impulsive. He no longer had to pinch his legs black and blue to force himself to sit in his chair and study for 30 minutes or more without getting up. He changed his college major from math to biochemistry and was glad he did.

In the joint Harvard-MIT advanced biochemistry class, he was smitten by a medical student at Harvard who always sat in the front row. She was the most beautiful girl he had ever seen. He wasn't sure how to get her attention, so he decided to sit behind her at each class.

* * *

Autumn turned to winter of Molly's senior year of college/medical school. She found that she enjoyed the schoolwork, tests, interaction with faculty, and relationships with patients in the hospital.

She kept her head down and worked hard. As her senior project, Molly applied for and was accepted into Dr. Brian McKenna's laboratory, a chaired professor at both Harvard and MIT in biochemistry and cell biology.

Professor McKenna was a genius. He had been awarded many lucrative grants by the National Institutes of Health, authored hundreds of peer-reviewed scientific publications, and was able to maintain a 10-person laboratory on the MIT campus and another eight-person lab on the campus of Harvard Medical School.

He was honest, forthright, hardworking, forgiving, and creative. He had only three rules for his graduate students.

"Rule Number 1," he instructed. "Everyone works in black pen. No pencils. No erasures, only light crossings out. What you observe is what you get, good or bad. No computer corrections, no redactions, no changes once you record your final data in the computer. Honesty through and through."

"Rule Number 2," he warned. "Work hard and don't quit, but I'd rather be lucky any day. Luck is a good thing."

"Rule Number 3: Keep all notebooks and computer data secure."

The focus of Dr. McKenna's lab was analysis and modification of new and old chemical compounds, establishing their properties and characteristics as well as their effects on cells both benign and malignant.

Molly learned that Aaron Katz was also assigned to the lab. By then, Aaron was a graduate student with a biochemistry major and chemistry minor. Molly checked out his medium height, dark brown hair, and bright hazel eyes. He walked with his shoulders back and a confident, ready smile.

"And what a smile!" thought Molly. "He's cute."

For the first few months, Aaron and Molly absorbed basic and increasingly sophisticated lab techniques such as expert pipetting, pouring agar gel plates and prepping them with study cells. They were exposed to experimental design, elution of gel matrices, chemical extraction techniques from plant-based sources, and designing and making basic organic compounds.

While Molly seemed to have a knack for cell biology techniques; Aaron was a wizard at the chemistry/biochemistry end of things. They sometimes worked on similar projects. Aaron was kind, patient, and humorous. Molly enjoyed his company. Sometimes they would get together for coffee or a movie, but nothing serious. They could spend hours talking with one another.

One Saturday just before Christmas, Molly came into the lab early in the morning to finish some work. She was alone in the lab. Suddenly the door opened, and Aaron walked in.

"Hey, how's it going?" asked Aaron with a warm smile.

"O.K. What are you doing here on this cold winter morning?"

"I'm putting this experimental drug through this liquid gel glass column to separate out any impurities, how about you?"

"I'm planting a new strain of leukemia cells on these recently-developed growth plates," Molly said. "I'm trying to see how well these Petri dishes with the new growth medium will support the mutant cells. I had to make some changes to this new batch and alternate the temperatures of some of the plates," said Molly. Her white lab coat covered her turquoise cashmere sweater and blue jeans. Her new black clogs made her look and feel a bit taller.

"Yeah, I have to check my drip rate and daily yield," said Aaron as he donned his white lab coat over his gray sweat shirt and pants. He stood there for a moment, as if making up his mind, then walked over to Molly.

"How about dinner at my place tonight?"

"Aaah, I have a lab report due," Molly said coyly, "but I guess I could spare a few hours."

"Spare?" Aaron's eyes signaled his growing attraction for this girl who he'd been admiring for six months now.

"Yes, spare. Happily, spare," Molly said. She tilted her head down but looked up into Aaron's eyes. She placed her warm hand on top of Aaron's as he leaned against the laboratory bench.

"Alright, then it's a date," said Aaron. He danced to the other side of the lab, singing to himself, opened the heavy door to the cold room, and walked in.

A few minutes later, Molly walked into the cold room with several new plates of cells that required a cooler temperature to suppress their growth. She would exchange them for others that needed to come out of the lower temperatures after 48 hours.

Aaron was standing on the other side of the room eyeing his glass columns, checking his production and quality.

"Hey," Aaron said, "Can you come over here for a second and look at this meniscus. I need a really accurate reading on this."

Molly walked over to look at the yellowish liquid within the long glass tube. She stood next to Aaron, put her eye close to the glass tube, and tried to gauge the rate of descent of the slowly falling liquid. She felt a gentle hand on her shoulder and responded by slowly turning to face Aaron. He bent down and kissed her.

* * *

Lab coats, goggles, sweat pants, jeans, arms and legs began to fly. A number of test tubes tumbled, a bubbling beaker wobbled, and several petri dishes fell to the floor. All of this went unnoticed until Aaron and Molly found themselves 20 minutes later on the floor of the freezing room.

Aaron did not want to let go, but Molly scampered up, got dressed, and scanned the room to assess the damage they'd caused.

"Holy shit," she said to Aaron. "Get up and help me clean this up."

"Only a couple of test tubes in one rack are cracked, "said Molly, her hair looking like she'd been through a wind tunnel. "One slightly cracked agar plate. I'll tell Dr. McKenna or Peter our lab manager that I dropped it. Luckily, the test tubes and plate are replaceable. It will have no effect on our experiment."

"Good," said Aaron. "All my glass columns are okay. One glass beaker got chipped but is still serviceable. I don't think any of the work has been compromised."

"Aaron, we have to get out of here," Molly said with an embarrassed smirk. She smoothed her white lab coat and walked briskly out of the cold room. She put the cracked petri dish on the lab bench and rubbed her hands together to warm them.

Aaron emerged from the cold room trying to hide his elation. "Well, that was quite an experiment."

"Sure was," said Molly with a smile.

"And that may only be Phase 1," said a blissful Aaron.

"I'll see you at your place tonight, seven o'clock?"

"Yeah, O.K. and I'll make sure the apartment is nice and warm," replied Aaron. Molly absentmindedly grabbed the cracked plate off the counter, threw it into her backpack, and walked out the door. She felt strangely light-footed. And it wasn't the new clogs.

# Affirmation of a Theory

New England after a snowstorm is spectacular. Snow hangs on the eastern white pines, the red pines, and the eastern hemlocks. The snow is clumped here and there like dollops of whipped cream.

Molly and Aaron, dressed in knit hats, goose down parkas, and boots, strolled mitten in mitten through Arnold Arboretum, the oldest such preserve in North America.

Established in 1872 with estate funds of a New Bedford whaling merchant, James Arnold, and designed by Frederick Law Olmstead, the arboretum boasts trails that meander through botanical collections and loop around Jamaica Pond.

Both Molly and Aaron had apartments two blocks away in Jamaica Plain, a neighborhood in Boston about two miles from Harvard Medical School. The old, diverse neighborhood, once blue-collar, was transformed during the 1980s and 90s into a student district with trendy shops, cafés, and ethnic restaurants.

"Doesn't it look like someone from above threw powdered sugar on those red maples and the northern red oaks?" Molly commented as they navigated the footpaths of the natural museum.

"Quite poetic for a scientist," responded Aaron.

"Hey, Aaron, speaking about that, I have something that I want to show you at my apartment when we get back," Molly said when the couple stopped at Jamaica Pond.

"Oh, yeah, what is it? A new puppy? A snowman you built?"

"No, but you may find it exciting."

"Now you are making me hot, but I'm sure it's all the winter clothes," Aaron said with his charming smile.

When they got back to Molly's apartment, she went into the kitchen to put on some tea. Then she came out with something in her hand that she placed on the great room coffee table.

"What do you think this is?" asked Molly.

Aaron peered at a cracked plastic agar plate smeared brown on the outside, with a brown color mixed with a clear medium inside.

"It looks like a dirty, old, cracked agar plate with you-know-what smeared all over it."

"Smell it," dared Molly.

"Whoa, whoa, whoa. You know I'd do anything for you, but I am not sticking my nose in that you-know-what!"

"Smell it, Aaron. What are you, chicken?" teased Molly. "Just smell it. Trust me."

Aaron bent in slow motion over the table. He took a quick sniff and stood up. He looked at Molly, head tilted and eyebrows raised.

"Well?"

"Chocolate?" asked Aaron.

"Yup," confirmed Molly. She proceeded to tell Aaron how she had slipped the cracked plate from their tryst in the cold room into her backpack.

"Two days later, I rummaged in the bag and felt something warm and sticky. When I pulled my hand out, it was covered in chocolate."

"That's disgusting."

"I had left a chocolate bar in there," Molly said. "But that's not what's important. Everything in my bag was smeared with chocolate. But when I picked up the cracked, chocolate-smeared agar plate that I should have discarded days earlier, I noticed that there was nothing growing on it."

"I planted L1210 cells, a mouse leukemia cell line, onto the plate and had placed it with the others in the cold room to decrease the rate of cell growth. When I shoved it into my backpack, sitting in there for forty-eight hours at room temperature or higher, the plate should have had extensive growth of malignant cells over the entire plate. Instead, with chocolate spread throughout and infused into the agar, there was no sign of growth at all."

Thoughts of Dr. Pierre Rodin, the children, and the cocoa farms of Cote d'Ivoire flashed through her mind.

"Remember I told you how weird it was that Ivory Coast was 'cancer-free'?"

"Sooo, let me guess," said Aaron. "You want me to believe that your malignant cells should have flourished at 70-plus degrees while sitting in your backpack, but the infusion of chocolate inhibited their growth."

"I'm not quite sure what I think," Molly looked at Aaron sheepishly.

Aaron knew Molly was brilliant. He knew she was an organized, quick-minded, think-out-of-the-box scientist. And he knew that many anticancer drugs were biochemically plant-based. He looked at Molly, eyes squinting, then raised his head and looked beyond her, and finally gazed directly into her eyes and smiled.

"You know, let's think about this together," he said. "Pool our resources. Give it some time to sink in. You're so smart. If you think this is true, it probably is."

Molly breathed a sigh of relief. Her face broke into a huge smile. She threw her arms around Aaron and said, "You're really great. Thanks."

Molly took a picture of the cancer cell growth plate with her cell phone, added a text, and then placed the plate in a zip- lock plastic bag.

"Hey, any of that candy bar left?" Aaron asked as he gave Molly a kiss.

# Eureka

Dr. McKenna sat in one of the laboratories along with Aaron and Molly, waiting for two of his brightest students to present the data that they had briefly talked about on the phone.

"Dr. McKenna, thanks for meeting with us this morning," Molly started off. "We'd like to talk to you about some new thoughts we had about chocolate agar."

"Chocolate agar? Chocolate agar has been around for decades," Dr. McKenna said. "It would be a strange surprise if you showed me anything significantly new about that."

Molly nodded. "As you know, Chocolate agar has indeed been used for many years in research for the purpose of growing cells. Also, as you are well aware, it has nothing to do with chocolate as we know it."

The three scientists knew well the history of "chocolate" agar. Certain difficult-to-grow organisms grow better on agar that has been enriched by adding sheep's blood to the medium. When blood is added to the agar and incubated at 35–37 degrees Centigrade in a 5% $CO_2$ atmosphere, the red blood cells lyse (break apart) and release the hemoglobin (red protein) from within the red blood cells into the agar. This gives the medium a *chocolate* brown color.

By the latter part of the twentieth century, chocolate agar was no longer used to specifically grow cancer cells, but instead, a generic culture growth medium is now typically used to grow cancer cells called Eagle's minimal essential medium (EMEM), a cocktail of sugars, salts, vitamins, and amino acids, red in color, developed by Dr. Harry Eagle in 1959. Other mediums have been used as well to grow certain types of cancer cells in a never-ending search for the perfect growth medium.

"Yes sir," chimed in Aaron. "But we wanted to show you something that involved adding actual chocolate to the medium preparations."

Dr. McKenna wrinkled his brow and said, "Are you joking?! You brought me here this morning to talk about Kit-Kat bars?"

"Not at all, sir," said Molly nervously. She described her experience in the Republic de Côte d'Ivoire.

"*No* cancer to be seen?" asked Dr. McKenna incredulously.

"Correct. None to speak of," replied Molly. She told Dr. McKenna about the serendipitous event that took place with her growth plates (sans the cold room "activities"). Dr. McKenna sat back and listened.

"Sooooo," said Aaron. "We ran a few simple experiments, and the data is all recorded in this notebook." He gently slid the lab notebook, written all in black ink, no erasures, toward Dr. McKenna.

Molly pointed to the lab bench. "As you can see, we have set up in front of you six EMEM plates. The first is the standard medium we use routinely in the lab. The next represents actual blood added to the medium. The next three are different supplemented mediums, DMEM, Plasmax, and Selenium-enriched mediums to promote growth or impede growth of malignant cells. And the last is EMEM infused with the best Swiss chocolate we could find."

"We planted our most virulent strain of L1210 malignant cells equally on all the plates," continued Aaron. "As you can see, there is growth.... some more, some less, on all the plates except the last. No growth. We repeated the experiment ten times. Same result."

Dr. McKenna sat in silence. The two young scientists stood without speaking, occasionally looking at each other wide-eyed, pale, jaws clenched. Their mentor stared at the agar plates on the laboratory bench, then looked slowly back and forth between the two junior scientists. Still silent, he picked up the lab book, sat back down in his chair, adjusted his glasses, cleared his throat, and began to read.

Thirty minutes passed. Aaron and Molly continued to stand, shifting their weight from one foot to another. Dr. McKenna finally snapped the lab book shut, stood up, pivoted toward them, and said, "Good work." With the lab book in hand, he turned and walked out.

***

Over the next week, Dr. McKenna agreed to let them both work on their project for two years under his grants. After that, they would have to apply for and be awarded their own National Cancer Institute grants. Molly would actually have little time for laboratory work over the next three years, maybe eight hours a week or less, as she would be completing a grueling clinical residency at the hospital, working with patients 80 to 100 hours per week.

"Since you will be working part-time on this project," said Dr. McKenna to Molly, I'll have to make room for another graduate student. She will be sharing your laboratory with you."

Aaron also had other projects that he was working on for his doctorate over the next five years, but he would be able to devote some portion of his hours to their joint venture.

Over the next weeks, the two young scientists had long discussions about *the* leading question:

What was it in chocolate that might account for their findings?

And how would they go about isolating that substance or substances?

Should they determine all the chemicals in chocolate and then isolate and test every chemical? After all there are approximately three hundred different known chemicals in the substance we call chocolate.

Or should they batch some larger portions of chocolate; for example, test the cocoa butter (that might contain half the sought-after chemicals) and then separately test the cocoa powder (that might contain the other half of the chemicals)? Of course, if, for example, they tested just the cocoa powder and saw no cell-killing effect, they might be able to eliminate as candidates all the chemicals in cocoa

75

powder in one fell swoop. Presumably, none of those chemicals would have the anticancer profile that they desired.

***

Molly and Aaron decided to relax for the weekend at the house that Mr. and Mrs. Katz owned on Cape Cod. It was a small, two-bedroom weathered-clapboard saltbox house with red shutters and white trim. A grassy lane bordered by hedges of ocean roses led down to Chatham Lighthouse Beach.

As Molly sat on a beach-side bench with a cup of coffee the first morning, a dense fog lay over the shoreline and ocean obscuring the rolling waves and tide. She could hear the lapping of the waves. The waves had always been there. The fog was covering the horizon, but it too had always been there. The small islands off the coast were hidden, but she knew that they were there too—had been for a millennium. And so too with DNA—its secrets were concealed, but they remained there and had always been there, she thought.

Later, nearing sunset, Aaron and Molly sat in Adirondack chairs looking out toward the horizon. The fog had lifted. The skies were clear, and the sun was still bright. They watched the flocks of gulls weave in and out.

"At first, they all seem to be the same," remarked Molly.

"But while they travel in groups," Aaron observed, "each one is different if you look closely. Each bird has its own pattern of flight, eating, and even mating, I'm told."

Suddenly, Molly turned to Aaron, Aaron turned to Molly, and at the exact same time shouted, "Test each one. One chemical at a time!"

***

Molly completed her three-year internal medicine residency at the hospital. Aaron completed his third year of five in a combined Masters/PhD degree program in advanced biochemistry, with strong application toward genetics. Molly was now entrenched in an additional three-year oncology specialty fellowship, where upon completion, she would be recognized as a board-certified medical oncologist.

* * *

Molly and Aaron dated for three years. They shared a passion for scientific research and were united in a quest for victory over malignant disease. They also shared a drive toward a trusting relationship. Aaron provided nothing but positivity, support, and encouragement. Because they had met while doing research, he appreciated and understood the highs and lows, the frustrations and triumphs, and the pure joy of the process of discovery. Aaron made Molly laugh, especially during the tough times.

Molly, exhausted, sat with Aaron one evening, while he listened to her frustrations.

"I'm not complaining, God forbid. But I began this journey as a hospital resident at twenty-four years old, having just emerged from 21 years of classroom schooling." Letting out a big sigh she continued, "For the next three years, I worked tirelessly--workdays of ten to twelve hours with frequent shifts of 24 to 36 hours learning to diagnose, treat, care for, listen to, console, laugh with, and cry with patients, trying always to *do no harm*."

The sick patient is most often frightened and leery of, angry yet vulnerable, worried and anxious about the very person who has been assigned to help them, their doctor. As residents, Molly and her peers were pushed daily from below by very intelligent medical students, and from above by demanding, sometimes self-absorbed, yet dedicated attending physicians and professors. It was made clear to the resident from day one that making a mistake was unacceptable.

The clinical training years are often the last chance for young doctors to digest the art of compassion, humility, truthfulness, fortitude, calmness, empathy, sympathy, directness, and good judgment. Many of those traits were already imbued in the young doctors but residency is a rounding out, a filling in of the cracks, a maturation of skills and souls. Special procedural skills are passed down, some requiring delicate and frighteningly difficult expertise.

"I also have to learn about caring for the patient who is emotionally breaking, sitting and talking to the dying patient, pronouncing a patient dead and then talking with the grieving family," Molly rambled on. "The enormity of the responsibility is terrifying."

Aaron listened. Molly mumbled, closed her eyes, leaned on Aaron's shoulder, and fell asleep in less than a minute.

# A Wedding Then Marriage

Molly and Aaron became engaged and moved into an apartment in Boston together. Six months later, they were to be married. It would be a small affair, only close friends and relatives. The wedding would be held at the Howland Manor, an old, 20-room sea captain's house, sitting in New Bedford harbor with a magnificent widow's walk that had a commanding view of the marina and the Atlantic Ocean.

Aaron's parents had been thrilled when he announced to them that he was engaged to Molly. "Perfect match," they said.

The reception would be held at The Blue Whale, a quaint restaurant attached to the Howland Manor. Molly's grandfather, Aram, and his Middle Eastern trio would provide the music: Aram Moravian on the oud, Harry Kashmanian on the drums, Haig Hagopian on the clarinet, and Christine Donabedian as the vocalist.

Molly and Aaron would be married by the Chief Justice of the Supreme Judicial Court of Massachusetts, the Honorable Howard J. McPuffin. Aaron's father had a business connection with the judge.

Neither Molly nor Aaron practiced their religion with deep devotion. They grew up regaled by stories of religious atrocities and had heard their share of holocaust experiences. Their belief and faith in God was shaky at best. They met with Judge McPuffin just to make sure they had the correct blood tests, their marriage license, and the requisite legal documents for the ceremony.

Kitty would be Molly's maid of honor, and Leo, Molly's younger brother, a lawyer, was to be Aaron's best man. After the reception, the newlyweds planned a one-day honeymoon and stay at the Chatham Seaview Hotel, the premiere hotel on the Cape.

The night before the wedding, Molly slept at her parents' home in New Bedford. On the morning of the wedding, Aaron awoke in their Boston apartment, showered, and put on his wedding suit--a three-piece, dark gray Brooks Brothers suit with cuffed trousers, a crisp white shirt, to be worn with a royal-blue paisley bow tie. The wedding would be an afternoon affair, to start at 3 p.m., but Aaron wanted to leave early from Boston for the drive to New Bedford to allow time for the judge to review and sign the necessary papers.

Aaron gulped down a cup of coffee, checked to make sure he had the rings, ran back to get his wedding shoes that he had forgotten in the bedroom, and ran back again when he realized he had forgotten his tie. As he prepared to leave the apartment, he saw two white envelopes sitting next to one another that Molly had left for him on the kitchen table. With trembling hands he quickly picked up the one that read, "For the wedding," shoved it into the inside pocket of his suit jacket and rushed out the door.

Aaron got into his rusted, dented Chevy Nova and made the one-hour drive from Boston to New Bedford. He was singing to himself as he drove. He had to force himself to pay attention while he drove down the highway.

"I've not been this happy and excited and nervous, in my whole life," he said to no one. "Man, I am about to marry my soulmate."

Aaron arrived at the Howland Manor about 1:30 p.m. He asked after Molly's whereabouts and was told by his parents she was in one of the second-floor bedrooms getting ready with Kitty and her mother. *And* he was not allowed to see her before the wedding. He talked with the restaurant maître d,' the flower people, and the cake people. He spoke with the manager about setting up a bridge table and chair in a quiet room off the parlor for the judge to sign papers.

At about 2:15 p.m., some of the guests began to arrive. At 2:20 p.m., Judge McPuffin came in, greeted Aaron warmly, and commented on what a lovely day it was to be married. Aaron directed the judge to the designated table and chair, placed the white envelope and a new gold Cross pen in front of the judge, and left the room. More guests were now arriving and taking their seats, and prenuptial music could be heard.

Unexpectedly, Aaron saw Judge McPuffin approaching him, red-faced, scowling.

"Can you come with me?" asked the judge.

Aaron glanced at his watch; 2:30 p.m. He followed as instructed to the room off the parlor, where the judge told him sternly,

"I am sorry, but I warned you that you needed the appropriate paperwork. I cannot marry you with this, the only paperwork provided in this envelope."

He handed the document to Aaron, who recognized his own birth certificate. A wave of panic washed over him as he frantically searched for Molly's birth certificate and the other documents that were supposed to be there.

"You mean that's all that was in that envelope? No marriage license? No test results?" cried Aaron.

"No, I'm afraid not, son. I cannot and will not marry you. And I am going on a trip to the Grand Tetons in the morning. My wife and I leave at 5 a.m."

"Could you please just marry us, and we'll figure things out later?" he pleaded.

"Absolutely not. I warned you," snipped the judge. Aaron was stunned.

"Could you please just wait a minute?"

He ran out of the room, passing the front door as Leo entered the room. (Later, Leo would say that he had never actually seen a person truly green before. He said that Aaron's head "looked like a ripe lime, dripping wet.")

It was now 2:45 p.m. The music was playing, and the guests were all seated. Aaron raced up the winding stairway and began banging furiously on the bedroom door. Kitty stuck her head out and said in an aggravated tone,

"What do you want?"

"The Judge won't marry us. I forgot the marriage license," cried Aaron.

"Yeah, right! Go away!" yelled Kitty and slammed the door in Aaron's face.

His suit was now completely soaked. He pounded on the door again.

Kitty opened the door a crack.

*"Will you go away!"*

"No, No, No," screamed Aaron. "Really, really. The judge isn't marrying us!"

"Stop bugging us," yelled Kitty, and she slammed the door again.

Aaron turned around and ran down the stairs, intending to beg the judge again. Leo stepped in front of Aaron, grabbed hold of him, and said,

"Whoa, whoa. Look, bro, I talked with the judge. I convinced him to do a sham ceremony. He'll go through all the motions, but he said you won't be legally married. You'll have to redo the paperwork and actually get married another time. Now pull yourself together. Give me the rings and go stand up at the front. My sister is getting married today, or something like that."

The processional music played, the guests hushed, and Aaron stood up front with the judge, whose face scanned the guests with a thin smile. Molly, looking gorgeous in her mother's white satin wedding gown with a short train, walked down the aisle. Soon, vows were exchanged, and rings were placed. Aaron heard someone say,

"You may now kiss the bride."

"But we're not really married," Aaron whispered in Molly's ear.

"Shut up and kiss me," Molly whispered back, flashing a big smile.

The guests retired to the reception area for wonderful Middle Eastern music, dancing, marvelous food, and wedding cake. Warm emotions were shared by all. While enjoying their small group of friends and family with a smile, Aaron couldn't stop thinking of his major screw-up. He felt tight. It was tough for him to keep the grin plastered to his face.

When the reception ended around seven that evening and all the guests had gone, Aaron told Molly that during the next hour or so of wrap-up, he just had to retrieve the other envelope. While on the one hand Molly was beaming, thrilled to be married to her soulmate, she could see the tenseness, the sadness in Aaron's expression. He and Kitty had a plan and he shared it with Molly.

"I understand," she said, with adoring, forgiving eyes. "I should have labeled both envelopes."

Aaron approached Leo and asked him to join him for a ride to Boston to pick up the "other" envelope. They walked briskly to Aaron's car, only to find that Kitty had attached streamers and trailing cans to the back bumper. Written all over the windows in white shoe polish was "JUST MARRIED." Aaron looked at Leo, and beseeched him,

"Get in."

It was nearing sunset as they drove up Massachusetts Route 24 back to Boston. At the fifteen-mile mark, a gray Honda passed on the left, honking the horn, while the smiling passenger gave a thumbs-up with one hand and held up a white cardboard sign in the other that read, "GO GAYS." Aaron and Leo smiled at one another. Twenty miles farther up the highway, a motorcycle passed, again on the left, with a beaming bearded guy riding on the back holding a sign that read, "GAY LIBERATION FOREVER." Leo and Aaron burst out laughing.

When they arrived at the apartment, Aaron grabbed the remaining envelope on the kitchen table, quickly inspected the contents, and drove the hour back to New Bedford. He had Leo recheck the contents of the envelope another five times on the way.

At around ten that night, they pulled up to the Moravian's house. Kitty's van was parked in front of the house, and Molly was in the passenger seat. She motioned for the guys to join her. When Aaron and Leo opened the van door, they were hit with the blasting sounds of the Grateful Dead at top volume.

"Got the paperwork. Are we ready to go?" asked Aaron. Kitty put the van into gear and shouted,

"We're going to get married … again."

Kitty had located the summer home address of the judge in Westport, Massachusetts, near Horseneck Beach. With the music blasting and everyone laughing and yelling, they pulled up in front of the designated house. There was a porch light on in the front, but otherwise it was dark. The four young people, still in their wedding attire, looked at each other, and Leo said,

"Are we really going to do this?"

Molly nodded once, turned to all of them, winked, and said,

"Let's go."

They exited the van, walked up the front walk with Molly gathering up her wedding dress train, as Kitty rang the doorbell. As she moved to ring a second time, a light went on inside. The door opened, and there stood Judge McPuffin in a long white nightshirt and a black night mask hiked up onto his forehead.

"What is this? Who the hell are you?" the judge demanded as he squinted against the light.

Aaron nervously explained,

"Judge, we're the couple you married today, but you really didn't, and we now have the paperwork dated today, so we were hoping you could marry us and go back to sleep and have a good time in the Grand Tetons."

The judge stood there for a long minute, finally raised his eyebrows and wrinkled his forehead. He shook his head and snarled,

"Give me the paperwork. Where's a pen?"

He bent down at a tiny table in the foyer, signed the papers, and said,

"I now pronounce you man and wife. Now good-bye."

The door slammed before any of the four could respond, and they stood there dumbfounded. Finally, Aaron grabbed Molly and gave her a big kiss, to the delight of the other two. They all broke out laughing.

* * *

By the time Molly and Aaron drove back to the Moravian's house and exchanged good-byes with Kitty and Leo, it was midnight. They made their way to Chatham on Cape Cod, about an hour away, laughing, recounting stories about the reception and what various people had said and done. When they arrived at the Chatham Seaview Hotel, where they had made reservations for the bridal suite, they drove around the large circular driveway and stopped the car in front of the entrance. They could barely keep their eyes open.

The first thing Aaron noticed was how dark the driveway was with virtually no outdoor lighting. He got out, walked up the front stairs, and went up to the front door. It was boarded up. His heart sank. He now recognized that the entire hotel was in darkness. Using his cell phone flashlight, Aaron could barely read the white sheet of paper tacked to the boards which read: HOTEL CLOSED FOR BUSINESS. PLEASE REFER QUESTIONS TO OUR CONTACT NUMBER ONLINE.

Incredulous, he stumbled back to the car, got in, turned to Molly and said,

"You are not going to believe this. It's closed." They were physically and emotionally drained.

"Holy shit," mumbled Molly. "What the hell should we do?"

"I don't know," said Aaron. "But we'll figure it out."

They decided to find a nearby motel. Molly began searching with her phone while Aaron began to slowly drive away. As they neared the end of the circular drive, a stocky man with straight black hair and bangs, wearing a security uniform and carrying a flashlight appeared from nowhere.

He approached the driver's open window and said,

"Hey, what's up, boss?"

"Well," said Aaron, and he proceeded to tell the guard (his badge read BILLY) everything that happened that day, beginning with the

85

envelope in the morning and ending with the boarded-up hotel sixteen hours later.

The little guard furrowed his brow, grimaced, tilted his head to the right, and then to the left, and said,

"Tell you what, Mr. And Mrs. …what's your name?"

"Katz and Moravian."

"Catsenmoronovin. You pull your car over there into that first parking spot. Get your bags and follow me. We'll see what we can do."

Molly and Aaron were wary, but they decided to take a chance. They could barely think.

They followed Billy to the front door. Aaron held the flashlight while Billy tore off the boards that were loosely nailed to the outer entrance.

"Follow me," said Billy.

He opened the front door, walked up the dark hallway, showing them the way with his flashlight. Aaron and Molly used their cell phone flashlights as well. From what they could see, the hotel was handsomely appointed— gold leaf sconces and beautifully framed paintings on the walls, plush carpeting, and attractive antique furniture throughout. They walked up a flight of stairs and went to the end of the hall. Billy escorted them into the largest hotel room they had ever seen.

"This is the hotel bridal suite," said Billy with pride.

He scurried around removing protective sheets off the chairs, tables, and desks and laid them in a heap on the couch.

"Wait here for just a moment."

Billy left the room and returned a moment later with two candlesticks, candles included. He placed them on a small table, struck a match, and lit the candles.

"Mr. And Mrs. Whoever you are, have a ball. I'll wake you around nine tomorrow with a couple of glasses of orange juice. Congratulations, and good night."

He walked out of the room, closed the door softly, and could be heard humming to himself all the way down the hall.

"Hey, Molly, sorry for such a screwed-up wedding day," sighed Aaron. Molly walked over and gave Aaron a big kiss, got into bed, blew out the two candles, smiled, and said,

"No problem. It was perfect."

.

# Bovine Undies

Following their one-day honeymoon, Molly and Aaron decided to stop by Eddy's diner for lunch on their way home. The place was packed. All the regulars were there jabbering away. Eddy could be heard working the customers,

"How you doin'? What's your pleasure? Comin' right up." Always with a smile.

Eddy's congeniality was well known among his clientele. He was the type of guy who would do anything for anybody.

"Always try your best to make the other guy happy," Molly quoted her father as they walked into the diner. "Always leave the customer feeling like he got a great deal," he'd say.

As Aaron listened to the lunch crowd, he couldn't help but notice a pair of panties, big enough for a cow, tacked to the wall behind the counter.

"Um, are those on the menu?" he joked as they sat down.

Molly laughed. "Let me tell you the story about those undies."

***

Urban legend had it that one late-fall afternoon, a thirty-ish-year old guy walked into Eddy's Luncheonette looking rather forlorn—rumpled white dress shirt, open collar, tie undone. He sat down at the counter, sighed, shook his head, and said,

"Cup of coffee, please."

Eddy served him up a cup of steaming black coffee and gently pushed the cream dispenser and sugar toward him.

"Rough day?" asked Eddy.

"Well, as a matter of fact, yes," said the young man. "It's like this. I took a job just a few months ago as a traveling salesman, primarily women's garments. I thought I was a pretty good salesman, and things were going just swell. I was making ends meet for myself, my wife, and my one-year-old son, but I made a big mistake a few days ago. A distributor somehow talked me into buying twelve cartons of lady's underwear, size 52. As soon as I made the deal, I knew I had been snookered, but it was too late; the guy took off and was long gone. So now, I'm stuck with a ton of unsellable, undesirable, outsized ladies' panties.

"That's a tough one," sympathized Eddy.

The salesman finished his coffee, got up, and went to the cash register to pay.

"On the house," said Eddy with a smile.

"Thanks."

As the young man turned to leave the luncheonette, Eddy said, "Hey, tell you what. I'll buy all those panties off you. What the hell."

The salesman couldn't believe his ears. They negotiated a price—cash, no questions asked—and the cartons were brought in and placed in the back room.

"Gee, thanks, mister, I don't know what to say."

The young man's smile lit up his face.

"Aah, forget about it," said Eddy, smiling back.

A month later, Eddy took 10 of the over-sized, multicolored panties out of the cartons and tacked them up at various places on the high walls and ceiling of the luncheonette. The ensuing questions were too many to enumerate.

A month or so went by, and the New England weather turned frigid. One December morning toward lunch hour, a farmer came in from the cold and sat down at the counter. He ordered the special, and while he was eating he looked all around the luncheonette.

"Hey, don't mean to pry, but what's with the panties?"

"Well," said Eddy, "Truth is I bought 'em off a young guy down on his luck."

The customer looked Eddy straight in the eye and asked,

"How many do you got?"

"I got 12 cartons, two dozen to a carton," explained Eddy.

"Look," replied the stranger. "I'm a dairy farmer out toward Taunton way. I got 200 cows, and it gets mighty cold out there in the winter. Those panties would be perfect to put around the udders of my girls this time of year. Are you willing to sell?"

With a wry expression, thin smile, and eyebrows reaching for his hairline, Eddy looked the farmer straight in the eyes and said,

"All of 'em? Why, sure, for a price."

The farmer and Eddy negotiated a price, more than twice what Eddy had paid for the undergarments. With negotiations concluded, Eddy pulled the panties off the walls and ceiling. The big fellow grabbed the cartons from the back room, loaded all of them in the back of his red pickup truck, and drove out of the luncheonette parking lot.

# Hope for Sale

Aaron painstakingly teased out the chemical makeup of raw chocolate over the next three years. He isolated all the chemical substances, organized the various formulas, and in his lab, reproduced the products he thought were essential to their project. Meanwhile in their spare time, Molly and Aaron consumed all the information they could find about the biochemical pathways that took place in cancer cells, as well as how those features relate to known genetic characteristics of malignant cells.

Molly would soon complete her three-year oncology fellowship program. She had spent most of that time seeing and caring for patients, but she was able to carve out eight to ten hours a week in the lab. She worked on various growth mediums for growing cancer cells in vitro (outside the body), and a chicken model technique for growing cells in vivo (in living organisms). She set up as well, the usual mouse models for testing anticancer drugs.

During her training, she had seen hundreds of cancer patients. No matter what stage their cancer was in, all had mixed emotions that included fright, anxiety, regret, anger, sadness, and more often than not, hopefulness, often seeking a miracle. Old, young, mothers, fathers, those with young children, those who were rich, and those who were poor—the great equalizer. Molly would sit with them and listen to their fears, and tell them that they had two, four, six months, sometimes one year to live.

"Am I God? No! Do I want to be? No!" she would say to Kitty when the two discussed medicine and their careers.

Molly talked to grandparents about end-of-life issues; talked to young men and women about the chemotherapy they would be receiving that most often destroyed egg and sperm production; discussed harvesting and saving their eggs or sperm prior to treatment in the hope of a cure, in the hope of starting a family one day—maybe. And how grateful they all were. And how could they show it? They brought brownies, cookies, candy, pies, cakes, and donuts into the clinic. As the patients got skinnier, the medical staff at the clinic got fatter and fatter.

Molly made house calls. Whether the homes she visited were large or small houses, tiny apartments, or trailers, she would inevitably be greeted with appreciation, a cup of coffee, and "How 'bout a piece of cake, dear, oh, I mean doctor?" Whether her patients were lying in bed or sitting in a Barcalounger attached to an oxygen tank connected by a long plastic tube strapped to their nose, there was often little Molly could do but offer kindness, sympathy, thoughtfulness, and her promise to relieve the patient of nausea, vomiting, and most of all, pain. She would collaborate with hospice to orchestrate comfort care measures.

"Not everyone understands the limits to a medical professional's abilities," Molly would, on occasion, rail to one of her colleagues. "The husband of one of my patients, who owned a large appliance store chain, once offered me a whole set of pots and pans if I would cure his wife. The wife of another terminal patient came into my office with a huge wooden cross hanging from her neck, threatening to light me on fire if I didn't keep her husband alive. Medicine can be sad, frustrating, and complicated."

Of course, there were the 20% of patients who were cured, — like the young man who came in for his yearly follow-up visit, fit as a fiddle, and proud to show his first-born baby pictures. Or the grandfather eager to share photos of a loving scene with his newest grandchild. Those were the lucky ones.

"Lucky or unlucky, I feel honored that these people let me into their lives, trust me with their healthcare, trust me with their future, whatever that may be," Molly told Kitty. "And then there is always hope. I often feel like I'm selling hope. With decisions to try treatment comes hope. Maybe another month, another year, another Christmas, another first communion, another graduation. And we doctors and nurses collude, with all good intentions, to sell the patients hope," Molly would say to her colleagues.

* * *

In the last month of her training, Molly was asked one day to consult on a new patient with pancreas cancer. All cancers were tough, but this was one where little advancement had been made in four decades.

Molly walked down the hall, knocked on the door, walked into the private hospital room, and stood by the patient's bed. He was a balding little man with bushy eyebrows, slouched in the bed and chewing on a Tiparillo. He smiled up at her as she introduced herself.

"Hello, Mr. Stein. My name is Dr. Molly Moravian, "she said with a grin.

Moishie Stein sat right up in bed with his wrinkled hospital gown half untied.

"I'm not really smoking this. Don't worry," he said, winking at her. "I just like sucking on the plastic tip."

"That's OK, Mr. Stein," Molly said, smiling.

"Me and the missus were at your Mom and Dad's wedding, y' know. How's your parents and grandparents, and husband?"

"I know you were," Molly said with a smile, "and they are all doing fine. I feel like I know you. My Grandpa Aram has told me stories of when you were army buddies."

"Yeah, you got that right," replied Moishie, grinning at Molly.

She sat down on the bed and asked, "How are you feeling? Pretty tough surgery that you had."

"OK," Moishie said. "But the food here is lousy."

He chuckled at his own joke; he still had a feeding tube in his stomach through which he was receiving his nutrition.

"You know you have pancreas cancer," said Molly.

"*Had*," insisted Moishie, followed by a grimace. "They took it out."

"Yes, *had* pancreas cancer."

"Yeah, and I know that ain't good," said Moishie.

Molly moved a little on the bed, getting into a more comfortable position to face Moishie.

"Well," she said. "You had stage two. That means no spread outside the local area. No distant spread of your cancer."

"I hate to interrupt you Doctor Molly, but how long have I got?"

Molly considered how to phrase her response.

"Well, you had what we call resectable pancreas cancer. That means there is a possibility of cure. The odds are not great. Some books give the chances of five-year survival at 20 to 30 percent. Others say less. With chemotherapy and radiation, the average survival could be over three years. I'll make sure you get the best treatment the world has to offer."

"Humph." Moishie paused. "Chemotherapy? Radiation?"

"First things first. Let's get you better from the surgery. Your recovery will take four to six weeks. We have plenty of time to talk about the side effects and the pros and cons of chemotherapy and radiation."

Moishie looked at Molly intently.

"Will I still be able to smoke my cigars and eat my borscht?"

Molly grinned.

"I don't know if I can condone your smoking. But you will be back to eating borscht before you know it. Twice a day if you want," she quipped as she stood to leave the room.

"Doctor Molly, I am glad that you are my doctor. Thank you. But hold on for a second."

Moishie leaned over, grabbed his wallet off the bedside table, and took out a card.

"Here, take this. If you ever have a problem, of any kind, just call me at this number." A little taken aback, Molly said with a wink and a smile,

"Hey, I'm the one who is supposed to be giving *you* a card."

She patted his hand and said, "Don't worry. We'll do this together." She turned and walked away.

As she walked down the corridor, Molly's eyes were moist. Every patient was a suffering human being. Every cancer patient had their lives flash before them— regrets, mistakes, victories, defeats. But there was something about Mr. Stein. Not just that he was an old friend of her grandpa's. Something about him pulled at her heartstrings.

# WWMD

The last Thursday in August found Molly working in the lab from early in the morning. Having completed her training the past June, she was now a practicing oncologist at the major cancer hospital in Boston, but she spent the majority of her time doing her research and teaching medical students.

She was completing plans and protocols for her next set of experiments, devising various vials of growth medium to test for superiority, as well as designing the next generation of *in vivo* experiments with mice. Aaron had completed his schooling and was engaged in full-time research as an associate professor of biochemistry. He and Molly were being paid from the funds generated by Dr. McKenna's grants. They began applying for their own national grants in order to finance their work.

Dr. McKenna had arranged for Colleen Whiteman to work independently over the last couple of years, using the same laboratory space as Molly, funded by her own grant money. Molly and Colleen had an arms-length relationship with one another. Each researcher worked on their respective projects, often sharing laboratory equipment, but clearly pursuing their own experimental designs. They would occasionally have coffee or lunch together in the cafeteria on the first floor of the Nott Laboratory, a new, modern building encompassing a complex of hundreds of laboratories on the campus of Harvard Medical School. Small talk mostly. They never fraternized outside of work.

Six months before, on an afternoon break, the two scientists sat together drinking their coffee.

"Molly, it seems like the work you are doing is quite exciting."

"We're trying. But Aaron and I are spending a lot of our time now applying to the National Institutes of Health (NIH) for our own grants to support our research. We have only six more months to be supported under Dr. McKenna's grants. By the way, not to pry, but who is supporting your research here at the lab?"

"My dad is the CEO of Whiteman Pharmaceuticals. He somehow convinced Dr. Summers, the administrative head of the Nott Laboratories, to allow me to work here under the company's independent funding program for a limited time, depending on the success of my project. Unfortunately, I think my time limit may well be coming to an end."

"Well, I hope not. Good luck."

***

Two months later, Colleen turned to Molly one afternoon and told her that the projects that she had been independently working on, a series of experiments involving gene transfer, had not panned out. She lost her independent grant status and was no longer funded. She asked if she could work under Molly's supervision. Molly agreed to allow Colleen to work for her as a lab assistant until Colleen figured out her status, how she could re-direct her career.

* * *

Months later, one afternoon about two o'clock found Molly poring over some recent data. Her phone rang while she was entering the last of her data into the computer. She could see that the call was from Aaron, and decided to call him back when she finished her work on the computer. As usual, she saved all information on a disk that she would remove at the end of the day and store in a secure place. She decided to put on some happy music, so she pulled out a Bobby McFerrin CD, one of her many unmarked disks containing music she had downloaded and placed it in the computer. But before it could begin, the phone rang again. Aaron.

"Hey sweetheart," Molly said, turning off the CD player to listen to her husband.

97

"Molly, you've got to come home. Now! We've been robbed. Please come home." The line went dead. Wide-eyed, Molly yelled to Colleen, "Oh, my God. I have to go *now*. See you."

She grabbed her backpack, slipped her work product into it, and ran out of the lab.

***

About a year ago, Aaron and Molly had moved to a first-floor townhouse in a more gentrified block of Jamaica Plain. About thirty minutes after receiving the frantic call from Aaron, Molly rushed through the foyer of her building and up the six stairs to their apartment. She could see the front door lock had been smashed, and the door stood wide open.

Molly walked in to see Aaron, head in hands, sitting on the kitchen chair with the cracked leg, the only chair left in the entire house. Through tears, anger, and emptiness, she scanned with bulging eyes the great room that now displayed only bare walls and bare floors; all the furniture was gone.

"Holy shit," cried Molly as the tears began rolling down her cheeks.

The other rooms had been turned upside down as well. Molly's shoulders slumped and her head hung low. All the new rugs and furniture they had recently bought on credit (and hadn't fully paid for) were gone. The artwork Mr. and Mrs. Katz had gifted to them—gone. The sterling silver flatware, bone China place settings and housewares received as wedding gifts—gone. Jewelry given to Molly by her mother, grandmother, and Aaron - gone.

Aaron and Molly visited the Moravian's in New Bedford the night before to celebrate Aram's birthday. They stayed over and drove back to Boston early that morning. Both went right to work without driving home first.

They wrung their hands, called their families, and sat there, still shell-shocked in an empty apartment. The house was a mess. Nothing of value was left. "They even took dresses, suits, and shoes," said Molly.

"Not that we have a lot," Aaron said.

"They took my engagement ring that was your grandmother's. That is irreplaceable," moaned Molly.

"I called the insurance company. They said they could come sometime next week or the week after," replied Aaron with a frown.

Molly's eyes were red, her hair was a mess, and her red cotton sweater was wet with tears.

"They took absolutely everything." She paused. "My mom said we could stay there, but I don't want to drive all the way to New Bedford and back. And besides, I left the lab in a hurry. I have to get back there early, to finish my data input."

As she thought of work, she went to see if the thieves had stolen her white lab coat and its contents. She went into her bedroom closet. There it was, rumpled on the floor. She picked it up and checked for her stethoscope. Gone. She went through the right pocket and was relieved to find her beeper, her patient information lists, and her prescription pad.

As she checked and pulled her hand out of the left pocket, out came a white business card. It was the one Moishie Stein had given her.

Poor guy, she thought.

"Hang in there," she said out loud.

She remembered him saying, "If you or Aaron ever have a problem …" She had a hint of a smile as she mused about Moishie.

Just then, Aaron came in and sat next to Molly on the edge of the bed.

"So, WWMD?" asked Aaron.

Raising her eyebrows, Molly said, "What? WWMD? What are you talking about?"

"You know. What Would Moishie Do?"

"Aaron, are you crazy?"

"Let's do it," said Aaron.

Frantic as she was, without thinking, Molly found herself pushing the numbers from the back of the card, and placed her cell phone on speaker mode. It rang and rang and rang. What seemed to be the last ring before it went to voicemail, a little squeaky voice answered.

"Hello," said the woman.

"Oh, I must have the wrong number," said Molly, about to press the red button on her cell phone.

"No, no. This is Sylvia Stein. I am answering for my husband."

"Oh, I am sorry to bother you, but I was looking for Mr. Stein. But I can call back later. This is Dr. Molly Moravian."

"Oh," said the voice. "He will want to talk to *you*."

A pause.

"Hello," said Mr. Stein. "Dr. Molly? I'd prefer a house call, but a phone call is pretty good too!"

"How are you feeling?" asked Molly, still awkward and scared about calling him.

"I could be better. I could be worse. I'm alive. That's good. But you're not calling me to see if I'm alive. I was just in to see you two weeks ago."

"Well," said Molly, and she told him what had happened at the apartment.

Silence. Then, "I see," said Moishie. "Now, doctor, listen to me. I'm giving the orders for once here. So, do as I say. I want you and your husband to pack a bag. I want you to drive down to the Ritz-Carlton Hotel downtown. Register there for three nights. And don't come back to your house until the third day. They'll already know to expect you. Got it?"

"But why--."

"Uh-hum. Dr. Molly, please let me give the orders here. Agreed?"

Staring intently at Aaron, Molly surrendered and said,

"Yes sir."

She heard a click at the other end. Aaron had already pulled out a travel bag from under the bed. Within the hour, Molly and Aaron had packed a bag, and were on their way to downtown Boston, across from the Commons.

When he hung up, Moishie made a phone call.

"Ricky," he rasped into the phone to Ricky "Too Tall" Stiletto, one of his foot soldiers. "I have a job for you."

# Inside Job

Aaron was in the lap of luxury at the Ritz-Carlton — the service, the food, the warmth and respect that its guests deserved. He had just completed his breakfast of French toast made of challah bread that had been dipped in egg, then coated with crushed Corn Flakes and finally doused in pure Vermont maple syrup. He was just finishing his cappuccino before heading to the lab. Friday morning, the end of a busy week, Moishie said not to return to the house until Sunday evening.

As Aaron wiped his mouth with the white, starched napkin, and began to get up, his cell phone rang. It was Molly. She left very early to get a head start on her lab work.

"Aaron, meet me at the lab as soon as possible. My disk with all my data is gone, and my computer has been wiped clean!" Molly said frantically.

"I'm freaking out!"

"I'll be there right away," said Aaron.

***

Aaron rushed out of the restaurant and drove to the lab, where he saw Molly crying at her desk.

"All my data. Years of work. All my backup. Gone."

Aaron put his arm around Molly. He worked on her computer, trying several maneuvers to retrieve her information, hoping that he would be just a click away from reversing this fiasco.

"It's no use," said Molly frowning. "Let's just go."

"Don't worry. We'll fix this," said Aaron.

Aaron hugged Molly, and in silence, they walked out of the lab and drove back to the hotel. They walked to a bench in the park across from the Ritz-Carlton and watched in silence as people fed the ducks.

"Why is this happening to us?" queried Molly.

"I don't know," said Aaron. "But I'm going to find out."

They ordered lunch in the room but neither ate much. Molly sat at the mahogany desk, trying to do experimental planning, but mostly bemoaning this latest debacle. Aaron sat in another corner of the hotel room at a smaller desk, going through the motions of working intensely at his computer. But he too stared out the window to nowhere, deep in thought, trying to put the pieces together. And what the hell are we doing in this hotel room anyway? he thought to himself.

Aaron was desperate. His mind was a jumble of emotions—anger, betrayal, vengeance, guilt. His thoughts were careening with names and places and theories and strategies and harebrained schemes. What next? They needed to get that disk back, soon, before someone had a chance to review it, copy it, or let it go viral. The compilation of Molly's work was on the disk, perhaps groundbreaking in nature. He sat and thought obsessively as morning turned into afternoon.

Who could the thief be, for God's sake? thought Aaron. His logical mind went through the possibilities. What about Colleen? She remained behind in the lab that Thursday, mused Aaron.

***

Molly and Aaron's laboratories were in the new five-story building, a modern structure made of concrete, steel, and glass designed to house nothing but research labs. The corridors were clean, white, with doors on either side of the corridor every twenty feet, the entrances to each individual laboratory. The pods of labs on each floor were loosely arranged into various research categories—cell biology, biochemistry, live animal research, genetics, hazardous chemical research, cardiac, liver, neurosciences and hematology/oncology divisions. The entire building was monitored and had finely tuned, ultrafast internet throughout. It was designed to have major computer, video, and audio cable networks as well as the latest up-to-date security system.

At about 4:00 p.m. that Friday afternoon, after he comforted Molly and shared his off-chance theories with her, Aaron headed over to the Nott laboratory building. He took the elevator to the basement floor.

This is such a long shot. I must be nuts, Aaron said to himself as he took a left out of the elevator and walked down the hallway. He passed seven doors and pushed the buzzer to the right of the eighth doorway marked SECURITY in big, black letters. The voice of a woman came through the speaker mounted above the door and said, "Security, can I help you?"

"Yes, it's Aaron Katz, I—" but before he could finish, the door buzzed, and he let himself in.

He was familiar with the vast office space designed with multiple cubicles, thick glass plates surrounding three sides of each cubicle. There were desktop computers at each station and a large multi-image screen on one wall. This monitored the twenty-four-hour activities of the entire research facility inside and out. He walked over to the fourth cubicle. He stood on one side of the glass plate facing a cute, young, short-haired blonde woman with a big toothy grin, black Chino pants, her white blouse open a bit more than regulations allowed, sitting at her station on the other side of the thick glass barrier.

"Hey, Bridgette. You look great, as usual. I came down to talk to you about a problem. I need your help." Brigitte had a crush on Aaron, but both knew where his heart belonged..

"Sure, hon, come around the glass and talk to me." Bridgette motioned with her right hand. Aaron smiled, came around, and stood on the right side of Bridgette. He could smell her fragrant perfume.

"Little closer, professor," said Bridgette.

Aaron told her the story about the stolen data.

"I see. So, you want *me* to help *you* check this chick out. Take a look at the videos and such, right? You know we have cameras all over this place, outside the labs but not in them, understand?"

He nodded.

"I can give you corridors, elevators, conference rooms, main entrance, and all exits." She paused. "So what lab are we talkin' about?'"

"Lab 309. Molly had to run out suddenly when I called her at about two-thirty," said Aaron.

Bridgette pushed several buttons, scrolled the various images in reverse, and grunted. "Let's see."

On the screen were four different images taken at various angles of the corridor, just outside Lab 309. The digital clock readout in the right-hand corner of each image showed three p.m. on the first screen. As the video proceeded, many scientists in white coats walked back and forth in the corridor, but the video was mostly boring, boring, and boring.

As the video flashed onto 4:10 p.m., Aaron could see Colleen Whiteman come around the corner and enter Lab 309, backpack over her shoulder. Aaron bent over and rested his elbows on the desk to see the screen better. Aaron watched the door to 309 open. At 4:35 p.m. on the screen, Colleen came out of the door, looked right and left, then walked down the corridor, around the corner toward the elevators.

Brigitte pushed a few more buttons, which gave them a view of the inside and outside of the elevators. Now inside the number two elevator, Colleen unzipped the larger compartment of her backpack, took out a round disk, held it up to the light, and placed it back in one of the smaller compartments in her bag.

"Sneaky bitch," said Bridgette.

She stepped out of the elevator. Bridgette pushed another button that scanned the main entrance and exit to the building.

Colleen walked out of the main exit about 4:45 p.m. Once outside, a guy of medium height with shoulder-length, curly, brown hair and sporting a trim beard and mustache, greeted Colleen. They exchanged a few words and walked off together.

"Know that guy?" Bridgette asked.

Aaron's brow furrowed. "Yeah, he's a friend of mine, or more like an acquaintance. Peter, Peter Bowman. Works on the fourth floor, 415, in genetics."

"Huh, Peter?" he said in a soft, cautious tone. "Wow, so she *did* steal the disk. Guess I know who's going to get a call from me, tout de suite."

"Duh, Peter Bowman?" replied Bridgette.

Aaron stood up. "Bridgette, I can't thank you enough."

"What are you going to do?" she asked.

"I don't know," Aaron said. "But thanks again," he said, heading for the door.

# Don't Worry, Be Happy

That Friday afternoon, Molly sat at a table in the Club Lounge at the Ritz drinking a cup of coffee, waiting for Aaron to return. Since Aaron left to talk with Bridgette, Molly had been thinking about recent events. And by the way, what *were* they doing at this hotel anyway? she thought to herself.

She had been working long and hard in the lab. Her most recent data looked like she was on her way to a breakthrough in cancer research. She thought they were really on to something important, something big. All her data was on that disk. Her computer back-up had been tampered with.

Molly shared not only an aptitude for numbers and probabilities with her mother, but also shared her mother's understanding of human nature, the foibles of other people and their often-devious inclinations. Growing up, her mother would talk to Molly about the unscrupulous tendencies of competitors and ways to "best guess" what other people would do or say in any given situation. But Molly had made a mistake. She had let her guard down for an instant.

Aaron suddenly came into the lounge, sat down and ordered a beer.

"You're not going to believe this," said Aaron, and he told Molly what he and Bridgette had discovered.

"But how do you know what she's going to do with the disk?" asked Molly, still very stressed.

"I have a hunch … and I'm waiting for a call from Peter," explained Aaron.

It's not that Peter and Aaron were best friends. They occasionally ate lunch together at the laboratory cafeteria. They had been out for drinks one time and had hot dogs and beers at a couple of Red Sox games. Aaron thought Peter was smart, honest, and a good genetics scientist.

Just as Molly and Aaron were finishing their drinks, Aaron's phone rang. It was Peter.

"Hey, Peter, Aaron Katz here. Sorry to bother you. Thanks for calling back on a Friday evening."

"Oh, hi. That's O.K. I was just heading out from work. What's up?"

"Well, it's a long story. Molly may have had an incident with Colleen yesterday. It would be important if you could tell me where you went after work, if you don't mind."

"Oh, wow, sounds serious. We just went for a quick drink at the Druid. Just casual. We then parted ways" Peter said. "My buddy and I had tickets for the Red Sox game last night. Good game too,

"You didn't happen to go anywhere else before the bar, did you?" asked Aaron.

"Hey, as a matter of fact, Colleen asked me to go with her to her dad's office the Hancock Building. What's this about, anyway?" asked Peter.

"Oh, I'll explain it all to you on Monday," said Aaron. "Look, you've been incredibly helpful. I really didn't mean to interfere in your private life. It's just that ..."

"Hey, it's fine. As I said, it was just a drink after work. Simple as that. I hope Molly is O.K. Hope those two work out whatever it is that's going on."

They ended the call and Aaron looked over at Molly. "There it is. Another piece to the puzzle. I feel like Columbo."

Molly, tensing her jaw, shook her head in disbelief at the betrayal. "I could just choke her. Come on, I want to check something. Finish your beer."

Molly went directly to her computer when they arrived back at their suite. She began searching Colleen Whiteman. After an hour of research a story emerged that made her stomach sour.

"Aaron, you have got to see this. You are not going to believe this."

Aaron scanned the information on the computer.

"Jesus Christ."

"A scientific investigation committee found that she had been tampering with the data from multiple projects," Molly paraphrased as Aaron read. "Her university research appointment was terminated. The National Institutes of Health was informed of her misconduct. Her medical license was revoked. Further investigation revealed that she had fabricated laboratory results going back to her undergraduate years at Boston College, as well as the time she spent at the University of Rochester Medical School. Due to her misconduct, over thirty scientific papers and abstracts had to be retracted. Colleen was banned from securing any further federal research funds."

Aaron had to ask. "How come you hired her? Weren't there any red flags?"

"The rumors I ignored at the time were probably true. Dr. McKenna was not happy when he was encouraged to accept Colleen into his laboratory. Turns out, Colleen's father must have gotten to Dr. Charles Summer, head administrator of the Nott Laboratory. Remember when Colleen told me that Whiteman Pharmaceutical Company offered to fund her research for a limited time?"

* * *

Carl was pacing the floor of his office that Friday evening when Colleen knocked and came in. Carl was the CEO of Whiteman Pharmaceuticals for the last five years. They would be in great shape financially had he not gone on a hiring frenzy two years ago. He brought in scientists from China, Japan, India, and Korea. He was now stuck with all of those salaries. His overhead was killing him. No big hit had emerged from his recruitment effort. He was anxious, nervous, upset all the time. He needed a big score.

Weitmein Pharmazeutisch was founded by Norman Weitmein in 1910 in Frankfurt, Germany. Norman Weitmein was a brilliant chemist, and as CEO, he led the research and development divisions focusing on diseases of the central nervous system.

After World War II, when he immigrated to the United States with his wife and three sons, he wanted a clean slate, beginning with his name, changed at Ellis Island. Within a few years, Norman Whiteman started a small pharmaceutical company in America, with the help of his sons. His youngest son, Carl, just completed his graduate school education. He placed Carl deep in the finance department under the watchful eye of his oldest and most trusted employee, Heinrich Braun, the chief financial officer. Norman didn't trust Carl.

While Carl attended Johns Hopkins University as an undergraduate, he blatantly broke the university's honor code during all four years. He commonly would take his examination back to his room so that every test for Carl was an "open book" exam. He got caught cheating during his MBA program at Boston University and was suspended for one year.

When Carl first came to work at Whiteman Pharmaceuticals, he was not happy that he had the smallest cubicle in the finance department.

Over the years, death, nepotism, and professional attrition moved Carl up the ladder to CFO. To date, Whiteman Pharmaceuticals had developed a number of "winner drugs." But Whiteman's income to debt ratio was falling without a logical reason. Creditors began knocking at the door. Carl knew he needed a winner.

His daughter had mentioned that she thought Molly Moravian, the brilliant young scientist with whom she shared laboratory space, was onto something big. A buddy of his from Johns Hopkins was on the grant approval committee at the National Cancer Institute. Guys like him knew who had promising grants and who didn't. Carl was told that the work being done by Colleen's lab-mate was stellar and had promise. "A possible breakthrough," he was told. He needed something, for God sakes, to boost his bottom line.

"Oh, hello honey. How are you? How's work going?" Carl greeted his daughter as she walked into his office.

"Hey, Dad," replied Colleen, breathing heavily and clearly anxious herself. "I got what you wanted."

"Thank you, honey," said Carl. "I really appreciate your efforts," he said. He placed the disk into his computer and waited. Suddenly Bobby McFerrin's "Don't Worry Be Happy" filled the room.

"What the--?" Carl shouted as Colleen turned pale.

* * *

"Aaron, Aaron," Molly had screamed earlier that morning. "Wake up, wake up!"

Aaron shrugged sleep away as he tried to comprehend what his wife was shouting about.

"She got my music mix," Molly chortled, holding up a computer disk. "I had put my Bobby McFerrin disk in my work folder by mistake!"

Colleen had inadvertently grabbed the wrong disk. Instead of what she thought was Molly's work product, she had snatched one of the music CDs that Aaron always complained about.

***

Colleen was fired and banned from the campus of Harvard Medical School. Molly and Aaron considered criminal charges but decided she had been punished enough.

***

Molly and her team were soon getting the engine started again. The wheels had fallen off, but she was putting them back on. She would welcome the ideas of colleagues as well as the work of competitors. However, Molly had learned reluctantly that the science community was not a close-knit one. She had been naive early in her career. There were fierce rivalries, large egos (concerned not only with science but the economics as well), vendettas, politics, and misogyny with which to deal.

The science, the answer to questions, the quest to discover the meanings and workings of life were the things that drove Molly. She shared Dr. Jonas Salk's perspective; when questioned about the

111

chance to become wealthy if he would only patent his polio vaccine, Salk demurred. When asked who *did* own the patent, Salk replied, "Well, the people, I would say."

Pushed a bit further, he said, "There *is* no patent. Could you patent the sun?"

# All Is Not Lost

Having driven home from the hotel, following their three-day stay, Molly walked up the front stairs to the foyer just outside of their apartment. Moishe had called earlier and asked her to stop by their burglarized home. Her eyebrows rose, her brow wrinkled, and a thin smile appeared, as she noted that the front door was repaired, closed, and locked. She used her key to unlock the door. When she walked into their great room, she couldn't believe her eyes. She took a quick breath inward. Every stick of furniture was back in place. Every painting was hanging where it should be on the walls. All their silver, China, and ceramics were back where they belonged.

She walked briskly to the bedroom. All their clothes had been returned to their closet. Their couches, chairs, and tables were all back where they had been—like nothing had ever happened. She pulled open the dresser drawers. Every piece of jewelry had been returned, even her engagement ring. On top of the dresser was a small, red velvet box, which Molly opened. Inside was a three carat, Marquis-cut diamond with two rhomboid-shaped diamonds on either side of the central stone. The diamond was in a beautiful platinum setting.

"Where in God's name did this come from?" said Molly aloud as she placed it on her finger. "Someone brought everything back." She stretched out her left hand and admired Aaron's grandmother's ring on her other finger.

"Everything!"

* * *

"Be in front of your house at ten sharp tomorrow morning. And don't be late."

The phone slammed down on the other end. There were no niceties to begin the call, but Aaron recognized the voice. It was Moishie Stein.

Molly knew Moishie Stein as the sinister figure who helped the couple regain their furniture. Since then, she mentioned to Aaron how she recalled seeing him around her father's diner, just watching and smoking a foul-smelling cigar.

The couple were still reveling in their good fortune when Moishie had called. "Go with it," Molly said. "Look what he's done for us."

So as instructed, Aaron stood ready at the front door the next morning at ten o'clock sharp. He watched as a gigantic, white Cadillac Esplanade drove up his snow-covered driveway. A small, bald head barely sticking above the steering wheel and a tiny, white toy poodle in the passenger seat furiously scratching, scratching, and scratching at the window would have made Aaron laugh under different circumstances.

"Get in," Moishie growled as he sucked on his soggy cigar. Aaron got into the back seat and greeted Mr. Stein. No response. The car reeked of cigar smoke.

They drove in silence for twenty minutes down to the bowels of downtown and beyond. Moishie suddenly swerved the car into a large parking lot tucked into a city block of old factories, warehouses, and smokestacks. He brought the vehicle to a stop at one of the dilapidated brick buildings, right at the bottom of some rickety wooden steps where the green paint had almost totally worn away. On the side of the brick building, in worn black, red and white paint, Eddy could barely make out:

HICKEY FREEMAN CLOTHIERS<br>MAKERS OF FINE SUITS AND COATS.

"Get out," Moishie ordered, unlit stogie in his mouth, brown spittle collecting at each corner.

As they walked toward and up the short flight of wooden stairs, Aaron, trailing behind, thought he noticed a slight limp in Moishie's gait. The heavy door, made of oak with brass trim, squeaked to announce their arrival. They proceeded through some sort of unoccupied warehouse toward an old elevator with wooden slatted doors.

"Get in," said Moishie. He worked the ropes, clanging weights and pulleys, allowing the elevator to rise to the third floor.

As they stepped out of the elevator, Aaron saw rows and rows of all types of men's coats filling the warehouse. Moishie waved his right arm in a big circle.

"Pick out anything in the place."

Aaron walked up and down the aisles for a few minutes before picking out a coat. It was a soft, dark gray herringbone cashmere overcoat with a black velvet collar, knee-length, single-breasted. It was the nicest garment he had ever seen.

"Put it on."

He slipped the coat on. It fit like feathers on a bird. Plenty of room.

"Take it off and give it to me. Let's go," Moishie ordered.

They went down the elevator and got back in the car, tolerating once again the incessant barking and window scratching from the front passenger seat. Moishie caught Aaron's image in the rear-view mirror.

"Driving through this part of town, near the harbor, reminds me of South Boston where I grew up," he said. "My parents escaped the pogroms, you know, when they were killing us, in Bessarabia--now they call it Moldova, in eastern Europe--and emigrated to Boston. My old man was a tough guy. Soon after I was born, rumors had it that he took off to New York City to join the Russian Jewish Mob. He left me and my older sister with a mother who had no money but a big heart. He sent money home for a spell but those funds stopped coming after a while."

"When I was nine, my sister, Gloria, came down with polio. My mother would take her back and forth to Boston Children's Hospital where they'd put her inside some kind of iron lung or somethin.' Within a year Gloria died, leaving me at home with my mom. She was all I had."

"But my mother died a year later. So, what does an 11-year-old boy do when his family ups and dies on him?

"That sounds terrible Mr. Stein."

"Yeah, the foster system wasn't exactly a good fit for me. As I got older, the few guys I knew started to rub elbows with the wrong element. I followed. I was one step away from the big house when I saw a recruiting poster one day. So I signed up."

By now the car had returned to the couple's apartment.

"Get out," Moishie said. He pushed the coat out the window to Aaron. "Look kid, that little doctor of yours is one in a million. I just gave her a gift, now I'm takin' care of you. I'm lookin' out for both of you. Treat her like a queen, O.K.?

The engine roared and before Aaron could respond, the big car was accelerating."

# Battle Plan

"The human body has thousands of functioning mechanisms that can go wrong," lectured Molly to the medical students, "any of which could lead a normal cell to convert to a cancer cell, and from there, the malignant process begins to grow out of control. In the 1960s, the results of studies from the National Cancer Institute and MD Anderson Cancer Center showed for the first time that the use of chemotherapy could slow down and decrease the tumor burden of children with leukemia. Over the following years, various drugs, combinations of drugs, and other hormones and hormone antagonists (anti-hormones), were shown to decrease the number of cancer cells in the body that were trying to kill the host."

"As time went on, it appeared that some combinations of chemotherapy, perhaps along with surgery and/or radiation, could, in some instances, eradicate *all* the malignant cells. In those cases, the hope was that all samples of blood, urine, tissue, as well as X-rays, scans, and physical examination would show no evidence of cancer. If the latter were so, the patient was said to be in remission. And hopefully, if the patient remained without any evidence of cancer cells for a long time, say five years, they would be deemed "cured," meaning they would live out the rest of their lives cancer-free. One-hundred percent of the cancer cells would be gone, never to return."

"But what about the patient that doesn't get cured, or recurs with their cancer," asked one student in the front row.

"Some of those sneaky cells somehow hide from the side effect-laden chemotherapy in well-hidden, protective sites such as the brain or gonads or bone marrow, called *sanctuary sites*. Those cells lay low, undetected, until they begin to grow exponentially as cancer cells do. The cancer cell mass grows bigger, spreading out in the organ within which they are hiding. They sneak out of that area and travel by way of the bloodstream. These cells then somehow find their way outside the blood vessels and implant themselves within other organs, perhaps many other organs. These malignant cells begin to choke the function of those organs with their show of numbers, in the billions. Mutations in the cells' DNA, their genes, induce insidious behavior, releasing harmful substances that benefit the growth of cancer cells, and destroy the ability of healthy cells to exist and function normally. The patient is said to have relapsed and, most often, is no longer curable."

**"What percentage of cancer patients are cured?" asked the same medical student.**

"Oncologists cure some patients (a remarkable achievement in and of itself to be sure), but by the first quarter of the twenty-first century, they had only been able to cure some 20% of advanced cancers, and very few stage four cancers (those that had metastasized to many organs of the body) with very few exceptions (those included testicular cancer and some leukemias/lymphomas). Oncologists worldwide competed intellectually and argued about which chemotherapy to use, in what amount, when to give it, in what combinations, and for how long. Having perhaps exhausted their efforts on a frontal attack, doctors and scientists began other approaches such as bone marrow transplantation, immunotherapy, CAR-T techniques, gene transfer and editing techniques such as CRISPR, and others.

***

Being an oncologist made Molly thankful every day to be alive. She had decided long ago that she would engage in cancer research as her way of giving back. The conundrums she experienced in Africa, the patients she had attended to and those that she had lost during medical school and residency, as well as the mentors she had, like Dr. McKenna, were all driving forces. To make any headway, she would have to have an overriding concept, a strategy, a plan of action.

She had completed her training as a clinical oncologist, but her passion was basic scientific research. This, despite her being told a number of times in school that "girls were not meant to be scientists." Susan Bloom had taught her daughter to be self-reliant, a critical thinker, a lioness in winter. Now she would use her education, intelligence, intense passion and devotedness, in order to fight this fight, armed with a well thought out battle plan.

Molly recruited a small, diversified cancer research team. She developed a manifesto of sorts.

"Listen up people. I've organized our impossibly complicated "Anti-Cancer Task Force" into six thoughts. Let's review the following slides:

1. Find the weakness: Like a general approaching a crucial battle, we must assess the enemy, pinpoint their major weaknesses, and develop a strategy to break their line at its most vulnerable point. The one (if this exists) root cause of every cancer must be found, and the attack strategy will be directed at this weakness.

2. Leave no cell unscathed: The treatment must find the enemy, wherever it is, and successfully destroy it with unrelenting force. 100% kill.

3. Flexibility—when the plan of attack is not working, one must be brave enough, strong enough, and honest enough to admit it, and then be willing to change plans/directions.

4. Stop the spread: While cancers are relentless, most often, patients do not die as a result of a local cancer growth. It is when those cells learn to break out, travel to distant organs, implant and infiltrate and destroy the functioning of those body parts, that patients die from their cancer. The successful strategy would be to prevent and stop the spread of those distant cells so that cancer indeed remains a local problem. Not a distant one.

5. Collaboration is a key element: Unfortunately, all too often, various laboratories show scant cooperation between each other. Research is a fierce competition, almost at a savage level at times.

There is often inadequate communication between bench researchers and clinicians, and often a fierce take-no-prisoners, ego-driven fight to "get there before the other guy."

6. Eyes on the patient: Know that regardless of the science, the focus must remain on the relentless, excruciating pain, exhaustion, nausea, vomiting, and abject loneliness that the dying cancer patient suffers while the doctor and patient wait, as the chemotherapy approach no longer works, and the unrelenting enemy inevitably vanquishes the host.

**"These will be our guiding principles."**

***

"Scientists working together?" Molly was fond of telling Aaron, sarcastically. "What a novel thought!"

She loved finding examples of historical figures who were on opposite sides of an issue and imagining how different history might have been if they had worked together.

"Take, for instance, Ulysses S. Grant and Robert E. Lee, two brilliant generals, fighting on opposite sides for different causes. They were both honest, trustworthy, courageous, but they were different men, different demeanors, came from different cultures, different heritages, different family structures, different versions of true grit. But imagine if they had been on the same side, colleagues, comrades-in-arms against a common enemy! *That* is what this war on cancer needs!" she'd tell him.

Molly was fighting for all of her cancer patients, as each of them fought for one more month, one more year, one more Christmas, one more wedding. Their battles to survive both inspired and motivated her. What she found remarkable about cancer patients was how brave they were. She would tell Aaron,

"How lucky can you get? Oncologists get to spend their entire day with brave people, those whose priorities have now come into focus, people who are indeed thankful for every day they are alive."

She once told a patient, "You are incredibly brave for enduring all that you have gone through."

"What choice do I have?" the woman responded.

"But that's what every brave person says," Molly answered

Never would she forget the patient, early in her career, who shared at an office visit a memorable poem, one Molly could recite by heart:


### *The Checkup*

"If you feel well,
You're probably O.K.," he tells me.
And I believe it on days when
I'm hard at work or play
Especially on days when the sun shines, strong
In a brilliant blue sky.


I don't even think then
of the runaway cells
that were stopped by a knife and
carefully controlled doses of
poison
..........probably.
I throw myself then into living,
working hard, playing hard,
and drawing the beauty of clear sunny days.


"If you feel well, you're probably
O.K.." I begin to think the month before the checkup,
And I'm thankful that the runaway cells did not kill me
the way they killed my mother before she turned 40

.....or her mother that same year.

I do feel well, I do feel well,
    I tell myself.
    But then the doubt creeps in because
    I felt well when I first felt the lump in my breast,
    And I felt well when the doctors told me, "Don't worry,
    We'll watch it for a month or two."

    By the day before the checkup
    I am scatterbrained.
    I will not think of the alternative to being well, but
    I cannot focus on anything else either.
    I take wrong turns, leave my belongings behind,
    Answer without thinking, listen without hearing.


    I will not think of the year on chemotherapy
    I will not think of the nausea, the constant chemical stench,
    the lassitude, the loss of my hair after the loss of my breast,
    the freaky lady drying up, with black and blue marks
    under my fingernails, the loathsome dependency, the
    loneliness, the terror-- and only wanting to be
    brave in spite of it all, and unable to be.


    I will not think of any of that.
    But tomorrow I will sit in the waiting room
    To have my blood taken and my temperature
    I do not want to be a patient ever again
    But tomorrow I will be a patient again.

And the flat, scarred side of my chest-
        that I keep covered most of the time,
        my own payment for survival-
        Will be looked at again
        To make sure there will be no problems.
        And I, who love words and the meaning they convey,
        Will be reduced to a tongue-tied patient
        With a six word vocabulary-
        "Yes." "No." "It's O.K." "Not bad."

        And everything will be O.K. because
        I feel O.K.
        But I will cry, for relief, all the way home
        After the checkup.

# Out of the Ashes

"In December of 1943, as the WWII Allies worked their way from North Africa to Italy, the German Luftwaffe struck a devastating blow upon Bari, a town near the "heel" in southern Italy," Molly said as she focused her laser pointer on an aerial photograph of the port city.

"The US Liberty ship John Harvey, destroyed in the debacle, secretly stored 2000 mustard gas bombs. This liquid sulfur mustard, as well as oil, was released into the waters of the harbor. The sailors who had thrown themselves into the harbor water were covered with oil containing the deadly agent. This poisonous mustard gas fused with the flames and smoke to form clouds, that covered the harbor itself and the town."

By now Doctor Takashi Nakamura was in tears. Once Molly had been awarded several lucrative grants from the National Institutes of Health based on the merits of her research concepts and successful data, she was able to hire an assistant. She chose Takashi, a brilliant PhD graduate student trained in cell biology from the University of Tokyo. Now, team members gathered around him as Molly stopped the presentation.

"My grandfather was there," sobbed Takashi. "He saw it all."

Between sobs he explained how his grandfather was a sergeant in the 442nd Regimental Combat Team, made up of Japanese-Americans, many of whom enlisted from American internment camps.

"More than 1,000 people—sailors, townspeople, and medical staff—began to have symptoms of mustard gas poisoning," he said as he regained control of himself. "They had shortness of breath, chemical burns, nausea, and vomiting, as well various stages of blindness. The Allies hid it all so that the German Army wouldn't know we were considering using gas—if they did. My grandmother said Grandpa was never the same after that. I never met him; he died of cancer. That's the main reason I chose to work with you on a cure, Molly."

Lieutenant Colonel Stewart Francis Alexander, a young chemical warfare specialist, was ordered by General Dwight D. Eisenhower to investigate the catastrophe. Victims of the Bari raid died from the toxic effect of the substance upon their white blood cells. Their bone marrows, the seat of blood cell production, had become aplastic (devoid of normally growing, developing blood cells).

"That's right, Takashi," Molly said. "In the 1940s, scientists at Yale University and Sloan-Kettering Institute found that a sister drug called nitrogen mustard could destroy cancer cells as well as normal cells. Similar drugs were synthesized. In 1949, Mustargen became the first FDA-approved chemotherapy drug. This set off a race by research scientists the world over to synthesize drugs and/or discover agents as components of natural sources that might be suitable to kill cancer cells but not the host, the patient."

"Thank you, Molly, team," Takashi said as he wiped his eyes and sat up straighter.

"In 1942, the first recipient of experimental chemotherapy, a male with advanced cancer, was treated with nitrogen mustard at Yale Medical School. It had some effect on reducing his cancer cells, but at the cost of significant side effects. The patient died soon thereafter."

"In 1947, Dr. John Lewisohn, at Mount Sinai Hospital in New York City, was experimenting with the anticancer drug, Teropterin, an anticancer folic acid antagonist drug extracted from brewer's yeast (folic acid is a vitamin required for many significant cell functions; Teropterin inhibited folic acid). He suggested that Babe Ruth, who had been diagnosed with an advanced case of nasopharyngeal cancer volunteer to be in the first cohort of patients to receive a combination of anticancer agents and radiation. While the Home Run King wanted to help pioneer modern cancer treatments, he of course hoped that the treatment would get rid of his cancer. It did … for a short while, only to come back and eventually kill him."

"In the 1930s, '40s, and '50s, brilliant biochemists strove to synthesize in the lab anti-cancer medications (chemotherapy). Even when these anti-cancer drugs were developed and shown to destroy cancer cells, their mechanism of action (how they worked) wasn't clear at first. In the 1950s and 1960s, biochemists discovered that most anticancer agents disrupted the metabolism and synthesis of DNA or RNA within cancer cells."

"From early on, the sources of many anticancer drugs have been found in nature (plants, bacteria, fungus, etc. Remember that Dr. Alexander Fleming in 1928 discovered penicillin from mold). Major, life-saving chemotherapy drugs have been extracted from plants such as the leaves of the Jamaican periwinkle, the Pacific yew tree, and the bark of the Chinese tree *camptotheca acuminata.*"

"In the late 1950s, doxorubicin (and its sister drug, daunorubicin) was isolated from a strain of the fungus Streptomyces, found near the Castel Del Monte (located in Andria within the Apulia region of southern Italy). This drug became one of the most effective chemotherapy agents for the next four decades. It was used to treat leukemia as well as many other different cancers. However, one of the major side effects, among many, of the latter agent was cardiotoxicity, temporary or permanent heart damage often leading to heart failure and death."

"Now you see what we're trying to achieve," Molly said. "Our research is born out of tragedy. Our goal is to make life better by curing cancer."

* * *

Aaron and Molly worked all fall, winter, and spring to isolate which of the 300-plus chemicals in chocolate might cause the phenomenon they had witnessed in the lab. Chocolate-infused Petri dishes, when filled with cancer cells, retarded the ability of the cells to grow or survive. As they laboriously tested each suitable candidate, eliminating substance after substance, their work finally paid off.

Theobromine, a methylxanthine (officially 3, 7-dimethylxanthine) is the major alkaloid in cocoa. Alkaloids are chemicals found in or made from plants that have nitrogen as part of their chemical structure. They often have profound pharmacologic and physiologic effects on humans. Various alkaloids had been shown to be anticancer agents in the past. Specifically, xanthines had been shown to promote apoptosis (programmed cell death), reduce cell migration, and arrest the cell reproductive cycle.

As Molly's work moved closer and closer to naming theobromine as the active agent that she was looking for, one thing bothered her. For every ten growth plates she used to prove destruction of her growing cancer cells, only eight or nine would show complete obliteration of the malignant cells. There usually remained one or two plates that had 1% to 3% of cells remaining after she had treated them with the test drug. She had tried changing the growth medium, adding various nutrients, or removing components from the growth medium, but each variation produced the same result. She tried changing the environment—hot, cold, increased oxygen, decreased oxygen—same result.

"Aaron, we've been working on this for months. No matter what I do, I can't get one hundred percent of cancer cells to die," Molly complained. She and Aaron were getting ready for an awards dinner where she would be receiving a scientific award for her work. She was frustrated, tired, and emotionally spent.

"I look like hell. I don't even want to go to this stupid dinner. I hate all my dresses," she said as she tossed aside her sixth try-on. She stood in front of the mirror, tears rolling down her face.

Half-dressed himself, Aaron walked over, stood behind her and held out his hand like a traffic cop. "Stop," he said. "You look great as usual."

He released his hug after a moment and plucked one of the discarded dresses from the floor.

"Here, wear this red dress. It looks great on you.."

Molly wasn't listening. She was picturing Aaron's hand in the mirror. A grin slowly emerged on Molly's face.

"That's it, Aaron. You're a genius. That's it. It's the D-isomer, not the S-isomer. It needs to be pure D-isomer!"

Every substance has a specific chemical formula, with only one formula for each substance. But if you have two molecules that each have the same type of atoms and the same number of atoms, but the atoms are *arranged* slightly differently in space, those two molecules are called *isomers*.

Isomers are mirror images of one another, and though they have the same chemical formula, they function differently. If you put your right hand in front of the mirror, the image in the mirror looks exactly like your left hand. But if you try to put that right glove on your left hand, or your right hand in the left glove, neither will work. The right glove and the left glove, while they look just like each other, are "isomers" of one another.

Usually, a substance is made up of a certain percentage of S-isomers (left) and D-isomers (right). Chemical techniques can be used to isolate either just the S-isomer or just the D-isomer of a substance.

Molly began jumping up and down. She ran over and hugged Aaron. She ran back over to the red dress that Aaron had picked out and tried to put it on while jumping up and down. She struggled with the dress, laughing as she put one arm through the hole where her head should go, and tried putting her head into the right sleeve. She started giggling and yelled "Help!"

Aaron had to come running over and tear her out of the dress so she could start all over. Aaron could not get Molly to put on her shoes because she was dancing all around the apartment. As Molly put on her makeup, she drew a smiley face on the mirror with her lipstick. Finally, with Molly half put together, Aaron kissed her.

"Come on, Mrs. Jump-for-Joy." And they walked out the door arm in arm.

***

In the lab, Aaron worked diligently to produce as much D-isomer of theobromine as he could to fill Molly's needs. She had to redo all of her experiments using just the D-isomer of theobromine, but the results were well worth the effort because *bingo*—no matter how she tested the pure D-isomer of theobromine, whether she used ten or twenty or thirty growth plates of cancer cells or different types of cancer cells, 100% of cells were destroyed.

On a beautiful spring Saturday night after Molly had completed all of her repeat experiments, and Aaron had completed the project that he had been working on, she asked him to join her at a quiet little restaurant in Cambridge. They sat down and ordered their glasses of wine.

"We haven't been out together for ages," Aaron reminded her.

He reached his hand across the table for hers.

"Wow, what a whirlwind these last few months have been."

"You can say that again," replied Molly. "How are you feeling about your work, our projects, about us?" She squeezed Aaron's hand gently.

"Us? The best. Would love to have more time for ourselves though."

"Ditto." Molly smiled warmly.

"Work? Going great. So, what's next?" he asked.

"Maybe baby mice?" Molly grinned at him as she sipped her chardonnay.

"Baby mice?" Aaron repeated, a puzzled look on his face.

"For the next set of experiments," said Molly. "Or maybe baby chickens."

"Baby chickens?"

"Yeah." Molly took another sip of her wine.

"What's all this talk about babies?" asked Aaron.

"Well, what about it? I have babies on my mind," she said to him softly, with a coy smile.

"Babies?"

"Yeah, babies. If I were us, I'd start off with just one at first," said Molly.

"Oh, yeah, sure, I think that's a good suggestion, doctor." Aaron returned her grin.

Aaron and Molly talked for a while longer about babies, but not too much longer. They both seemed to want to get the check and go home. Molly definitely did not think of cells that night. And Aaron definitely did not think about biochemistry. Genes, maybe, but doubtful.

# Stuff Happens

Having proved that theobromine destroyed cancer cells within the growth medium used in her *in vitro* investigations, Molly directed her efforts toward *in vivo* experiments involving live organisms. Instead of mice or rats, Molly and Takashi teamed up to test theobromine using the PDcE model (patient-derived chicken egg tumor model).

In the lab, Molly sat on a lab bench, while Takashi Nakumura explained the technique to Jeffrey Shaw, a medical student that Molly hired for the summer.

"These experiments use fertilized chicken eggs to grow cancer cells," he explained. "With a scalpel, a quarter-inch square window is cut in the chicken eggshell. Just beneath the surface of the shell is a membrane containing many blood vessels that surrounds the chick embryo. Can you see that?"

"Yes," said Jeffrey.

"Active cancer cells can be transplanted through the window onto the membrane, and within three to four days, a tumor mass grows. This method is often better for research as opposed to using a mouse, which can take from two to six weeks to produce a visible and measurable transplanted tumor."

In addition, Molly had begun a collaboration with the surgical department, asking Dr. Samantha Patel, surgical oncologist, to take a lead in the project. Samantha had been a classmate of Molly's at Harvard Medical School. She was smart, hardworking, reliable, a good communicator, and interested in participating in cancer research. She worked with the hospital ethics committee about rules and regulations for using human specimens and animal models.

"The PDcE model allows for high transplantation efficiency for individual patient cancer cells. Cancer development and formation within the egg model is quick," explained Takashi. "The nutrient-rich membrane develops and surrounds the embryo by day three following egg fertilization. As a cancer takes three to four days to grow onto this membrane, the malignant cells help to make and recruit other necessary components from the membrane that the cancer needs to grow. Since a chick embryo hatches in about twenty-one days, there is an eight-to-ten-day window of time to perform any experiments on the transplanted cancers."

"So let's make sure we're all on the same page," Molly said to Takashi and Jeffrey. "We started with 200 eggs. Only 180 could be used due to damage of some sort. Takashi, you have nine groups of ten models each and will give different doses of various known chemotherapy drugs to the tumors that have grown. You'll then sacrifice the embryos at day 19 to make your measurements. Right?"

"Exactly," said Takashi.

"And Jeffrey, do you feel comfortable with the technique?"

Jeffrey glanced up from his note-taking.

"Yes, I think I have it down."

Molly continued. "Jeffrey, you have eight groups of ten eggs with one control group. You will infuse into the eight groups varying doses of *theobromine*, at various time intervals and in different environments including heat, cold, high and low humidity. The control group will be left alone to grow on its own."

"Right," Jeffrey said.

"And you are having no trouble injecting the main membrane blood vessel with the drug?"

"No, I've got the hang of it. Dr. Nakamura is a good teacher," he said, looking over and smiling at Takashi. "But …"

"But what?" Molly asked.

"Well, it's Monday today. Next weekend is the fourth of July. All the labs will be closed. I was wondering whether I could take tomorrow off. I sort of promised my girlfriend that I'd take her to Cape Cod for the day."

He gave Molly a sheepish look. "I'll be back for Wednesday, Thursday, and Friday to sacrifice the embryos, remove the tumors, and make my measurements."

"Will that give you enough time?" asked Molly.

"Yes, I think so." Jeffrey shifted from one foot to the other.

Molly looked intently at the young student for a moment.

"I guess so," she said reluctantly, cocking her head, looking at the calendar on the wall. "As long as you get your work done. Looks like Day 21 is Friday."

"O.K." Molly said, standing up. "Let's hope the results look good."

Molly stayed late as usual. She promised herself (and her husband) she would not work this Saturday and Sunday. She was going to take a long weekend with Aaron.

* * *

Molly was humming to herself the following Monday morning as she took out her keys to unlock the door to the laboratory. She had just enjoyed a long, relaxing weekend with Aaron.

"Jeffrey, you're here bright and early," she greeted the medical student as he ran up to her.

"Well, Doctor Moravian, I have something to tell you. It's important," he said looking pale as Molly put the keys in the lock.

"Uh-huh," Molly said absentmindedly. "Well, if you could just ..."

As she opened the door, all Molly could see were dozens of yellow chicks—on the shelves, the workbenches, refrigerators, and incubators; they covered every desk and chair in the lab, and they were all over the floor. The lab smelled like a chicken coop. Molly heard nothing but a cacophony of peeping, peeping, peeping of over 100 chicks.

"Oh, my God!" she yelled.

"What the hell happened here?!" She shot a furious glance at Jeffrey. "In my office," she yelled.

Jeffrey proceeded to explain to Molly how a world-renowned cancer research lab had been converted into a filthy chicken coop.

"So, just so I have this straight," Molly all but growled. "You drove to Cape Cod with your girlfriend, parked your car on the sand dunes which is illegal, got your car stuck in the sand to the point where you had to climb out the windows, had to be towed from the dunes at midnight, got arrested by the state police, spent two nights in jail, did not make it back in time to carry out your responsibilities in *my* cancer research lab, and ruined two months of experiments that Dr. Takashi and I have been working on."

Jeffrey looked like he was about to piss in his pants.

"Yes, ma'am," he squeaked.

"And you didn't have the sense, the decency to call me?"

Jeffrey hung his head and offered to clean up the mess.

Molly turned abruptly and walked to her office. She spent the afternoon in her office, frustrated and furious. She would have to start the experiments all over again, she thought, as she plucked a bunch of chicken feathers out of her hair.

At the end of the afternoon, Jeffrey approached Molly in her office. He stood in the doorway until she raised her head.

"Dr. Moravian, I caught all the chicks. and put them in cages."

"Uh-huh."

"I swept the floor and wiped down all the counters."

"Uh-huh."

"And I vacuumed up all the feathers and sterilized all the equipment. Things should be all set," Jeffrey said.

Molly stuck her right arm out straight and pointed to the exit door of the lab.

"Now take all the chickens, get out, and don't come back!"

* * *

Molly was so disgusted that she went home shortly after firing Jeffrey. Aaron, who had stuck around to finish cleaning up, was whipped when he arrived a few hours later.

"What a shitty job," he complained as he plopped down after a long shower.

Molly looked at him a moment, then burst out laughing.

"What?" Aaron asked.

"Shitty job?" Now Molly was almost roaring with laughter. "Shitty job? Let me tell you about a shitty job."

As the tension of the long day drained from her, Molly giggled as she recalled her first job after high school, months before she went to Africa.

***

Molly arrived promptly at 9 a.m. She wanted to make a good impression. The lawyer's office was in a small gray, wooden clapboard house, two streets back from Main Street.

"So, you're Molly," said. Mr. Schnoible. "I've heard good things about you. I hope they are true."

She looked up to see that the boss was a small man with a pot belly, who was wearing a dark gray suit with a red bow tie, and black-and-white saddle shoes. His graying horseshoe of hair surrounded a shiny bald head. Scotch-taped half glasses sat at the end of his nose, so it always seemed like he was looking down at you no matter how tall he was or how tall you were.

Molly took some deep breaths. She forced a smile. She wanted to do well and wanted things to go just right on this first day. She said hello and that she was happy to be working there.

"As long as you behave yourself, and you do as you're told, you and I will get along just fine. We keep a tight ship around here," her boss said sternly. He walked over to the coffee pot and poured himself a cup of black coffee into an old chipped mug. As he lifted the mug toward his lips, the top of the mug hit the edge of the coffee machine. Half the dark liquid spilled on the counter. Mr. Schnoible shook his head, made a grunting noise, and walked back to his office causing a trail of brown spots on the floor from the kitchen to his desk.

The day went by rather quickly. Molly answered the phone and did the filing, trying not to make any mistakes. It was quiet. Only one or two clients had come and gone. At one point, Molly peered into Mr.

135

Schnoible's office where she saw him leaning back in his chair, suit coat off revealing thick red suspenders. He was cutting his fingernails with the largest pair of sheers that she had ever seen.

It was getting late in the afternoon. Molly did not know exactly what time she was expected to go home. She wanted them to think that she was a good, tidy, hard worker. As the day grew to a close, Molly's stomach began to hurt. As the minutes passed, she felt increasingly bloated. Was it the Chinese food she had the night before? She went into the bathroom, sat on the toilet, and could not get up. She really had to go. She remained seated until her stomach finally felt better. She got up and flushed the toilet. While she washed her hands, she noticed a small piece of white paper on the floor with a piece of Scotch tape attached to it. She dried her hands, picked up the paper, and turned it over. In block print, it read, Hold Handle Down For Ten Seconds Before Flushing. She definitely did not do that.

Molly looked in horror as she noticed the water slowly rising in the toilet. "No, no, no, no, no!" she panic-whispered.

She quickly pushed the handle down and up and down and up and down … to no avail. The water continued to rise. The bowl was about to overflow. She looked frantically for a plunger. Nowhere in sight. Water cascaded over the rim, onto the floor, and ran quickly toward the bathroom door.

"Holy shit," Molly whispered.

She could not suppress her rapid breathing. Sweat began pouring down her face. Water seeped out the door into the foyer. She tried to stop it with her feet. Her new flats were now soaked, and her white ankle socks were soggy and discolored.

"Hey, is everything all right in there?" yelled Shirley from the other side of the door. Next came a deeper, louder voice.

"What the hell is happening in there? Hey, you, come out of there!"

Molly did not know what to do.

"Hey. Oh shit. Come out of there you little …," screamed Mr. Schnoible.

Molly fumbled with the lock. She struggled to open the door a crack and out whooshed a torrent of water, traveling fast now, into Mr. Schnoible's office, into Shirley's office, and into the filing room. Rushing water, with office papers floating in it, flowed toward the front door.

Opening the door further Molly could see Mr. Schnoible standing there, purple-faced, both hands in the air, a plunger in his right hand, as water covered his saddle shoes. Both pant legs were immersed in water two inches above the cuffs of his suit trousers. Shirley stood five feet away, files dropping out of her hands. Her mascara ran down her face, her makeup was smeared, and the corners of her mouth drooped. It looked like she had no feet as her high heels were submerged above her stockinged ankles.

There is only one thing to do, thought Molly to herself. Shoulders back, head high, eyes forward, Molly sloshed out of the bathroom, continued straight past Mr. Schnoible, splashed around Shirley, and made her way out the front door. It was dark as she squished her way home.

"Now that was one shitty day!" Molly said as she walked up her drive.

# Kitty's Tale

Kitty completed her physician assistant degree and now worked with Dr. Jane Brewster, a sports medicine physician. Jane was a buxom redhead who wore her hair in a bun at the top of her head. She wore tortoiseshell glasses and had a rosy but smooth complexion, strong arms and legs, and a killer smile. In addition to office and hospital work, Kitty and her boss attended to youth athletic leagues as well as collegiate athletes in the Boston suburbs. Dr. Brewster, appreciating Kitty's excellent skills, bedside manner, and growing knowledge of the field, allowed Kitty to do lots on her own. She trusted Kitty.

Not infrequently, Dr. Brewster and Kitty would work late nights together—hockey games, basketball games, and hospital emergency rooms. After a long night, several months after they'd started working together, the doctor invited Kitty over to her house for a well-deserved drink. She lived in Wellesley Hills, in a large brick house, antebellum Southern style with four tall white pillars in front, a three-car garage, with a generous screened porch. The property was expansive, back and front, with lush garden beds designed with pachysandra, hydrangeas, rhododendron, and azaleas. The yard was adorned with tall maples, giant elms, healthy magnolias, and red and pink dogwoods. Walking from the front yard to the back there were multi-level grassy landings built into the design of the yard by railroad-tie stairways and stone walls of varying heights.

Dr. Brewster, still in her late thirties, lived alone. Drinks in hand, they sat in the den, Jane on the white sofa and Kitty comfortable in a Whitman overstuffed armchair. As they sat by the fire, they discussed the day and talked about some difficult cases. They also shared some of their prior athletic experiences and sports highlights. Kitty told some funny stories about when she was the only girl in Little League. Jane talked about her heyday in college lacrosse.

At one point, as they were chatting and laughing, Jane said, "Hey, Kitty, why don't you come over and sit on the couch."

Kitty turned quiet and looked down at the red-and-green Persian rug. She had a funny feeling in her chest that she had never had before. Kitty looked up and saw Jane grinning with a fine line of a smile, pink glossy lipstick, a coy expression on her face. Jane scooted over a bit to the right on the couch to make room, and patted the cushion to her left, beckoning Kitty to sit down next to her. Kitty hesitated for a moment, a bit flushed, and got up slowly out of the chair. She walked slowly around the coffee table past the coffee table books with shiny covers revealing scenes from the Galapagos Islands on one, Billie Jean King on another, and a poetry book revealing a gorgeous photograph of New England in its autumn splendor on yet another. Kitty cautiously sat down beside Jane Brewster, MD.

Kitty was excited several months ago when she told Molly that she had moved in with Jane. Molly was happy for her best friend.

"Kitty, I am so glad that you have a partner who you can share your life with. And Jane is such a great person." But best of all, Molly could see that Kitty and Jane loved one another deeply.

But one day, things fell apart.

"What? You have cancer?" asked Dr. Jane Brewster. She had been stirring the soup on the stove. She dropped the spoon on the floor.

"Yeah, that's what the doctor said. Melanoma of the labia," cried Kitty. Tears welled up in the eyes of both women. Jane walked over to Kitty and gave her a long hug.

"Tell me what happened," said Jane.

***

Kitty introduced Molly ("oncologist and long-time friend") to Dr. Schneider as they sat down in front of his office desk. They smiled weakly at one another.

"So, Ms. McGee—

"You can call me Kitty," Kitty interrupted.

"So, Kitty, the biopsy of your left labia shows cancer, melanoma, I'm afraid," Dr. Schneider told her bluntly. He looked over his oversized glasses to gauge her reaction as he read from the report in his hands.

"But I thought you get melanoma in sun-exposed areas, and that it mostly affects people who live in the Sunbelt. Are you sure the diagnosis is correct?" asked Kitty, her expression hopeful.

"Actually, one can develop melanoma in any area of the body; it can spread to any organ." Dr. Schneider paused to give Kitty a moment to process this new information.

"We sent the biopsy specimen for a second opinion to the best pathology department in Boston that specializes in melanoma. Unfortunately, they confirmed the diagnosis of melanoma."

Kitty slumped back in her chair.

"We worry about how deep melanoma grows into your skin. Yours is deep. I am referring you to an oncologist. They will help you," the doctor said dryly, almost looking beyond Kitty.

"Well, as I said, I've brought my oncologist with me," said Kitty as she looked at Molly.

"Do you know of Dr. Molly Moravian?" He glanced up at Molly and the two physicians simultaneously nodded their heads at one another in brief acknowledgment.

"But, Ms. McGee, I am also concerned about that lump in your left groin," said Dr. Schneider. His facial expression betrayed nothing.

"You mean that hernia I have from working out?"

"Ms. McGee, I think, but I don't know yet, that the lump may be related to your melanoma. It may be an enlarged lymph node with cancer inside it. You will need a biopsy of that lump, blood work, X-rays, and scans," he said bluntly.

"Jesus Christ," said Kitty, face flushed and turning toward Molly.

"We'll talk about it," Molly winked at Kitty. Kitty heard little to nothing of what the doctor said after that.

Molly knew the drill. She knew that her friend was going to be told that she had stage 3 or perhaps stage 4 melanoma. She knew that Kitty's biopsy of her left groin lump would likely reveal a cancerous lymph node.

***

Kitty and Molly left the office having been given a referral to the oncologist. They got in the car and sat in silence. Kitty took a deep breath and breathed out slowly through pursed lips.

"I think we should wait to see what your oncologist says," Molly said softly.

"What do you mean? You're not going to be my oncologist?" Kitty wanted Molly to be her oncologist but Molly declined. As health care providers, they both knew that Kitty would require a physician whose objectivity would not be clouded by their friendship.

"Well what do you think the oncologist is going to say?"

"Kitty, we can wait until we get home to talk about this." Molly took Kitty's hand in hers.

"No, Molly," Kitty said, staring straight ahead through the windshield. "I want to know what I'm in for."

Melanoma of the skin, like all cancers, was a formidable enemy. It grew fast, it could spread like wildfire, and the prognosis was abysmal. Chemotherapy, radiation, and surgery had done little to stop it.

"The oncologist may talk to you about surgery to remove your cancer, followed by anti-melanoma intravenous treatment, either targeted therapy, immunotherapy or both."

For years, scientists studying immunotherapy had tried to manipulate T-lymphocytes, the cells in the body that destroy any foreign cells, including cancer cells. The goal was to drive these "killer" lymphocytes toward mortally wounding cancer that was invading the system. Progress had been made, but not enough. Cells became resistant. Many of the cancer cases did not have that very specific element by which the immunotherapy was designed to work.

"Sounds harsh."

"You're tough. You'll get through it. Intravenous immunotherapy is often easier than chemotherapy. I won't be your official oncologist, but I will be with you, mind and body, all the way."

"All the way where?" Kitty asked as the tears continued to flow.

Molly gently squeezed Kitty's hand. She grabbed some tissues from the glove compartment and handed them to Kitty. She took some for herself as well.

"How the fuck am I going to do this? Thank God I have you and Jane in my life," Kitty said, blowing her nose, turning to face Molly.

"Every step of the way. You know I love you like a sister."

Kitty would have to make decisions, weigh the pros and cons, risks versus benefits, all with little knowledge of melanoma—its viciousness and poor rates of survival, with and without treatment.

"I'm suddenly starting to see my life flash before my eyes. What about all the plans we've made?"

"Hey, how about we go home so you can be with Jane and talk to her about all this?"

"Yeah. I guess so, "sighed Kitty. "She is going to freak out."

"No, she is going to show you the love and support that she has always shown you." Molly started the car and the two friends drove toward home.

* * *

Kitty sat down at the kitchen table with Jane. She shared what Dr. Schneider told her as well as Molly's assessment.

"Maybe it's all a mistake," said Kitty with a hopeful grin. "Maybe that stupid doctor doesn't know what he's talking about."

Jane placed her warm hand on top of Kitty's. She then stood up, came around the table and put her arms around Kitty. She gently kissed her lover on the top of her head.

142

"Why don't we have a nice bowl of soup?" she murmured. "I agree with Molly. We can continue to discuss this, and we'll see what the oncologist has to say. I'll go with you. I'll be there for you in whatever capacity you need me. Forever. I love you."

She fought back tears as she walked over to the stove and began to ladle soup into bowls.

***

About six months after Kitty had her scans and surgery for malignant melanoma Molly came, as she did every two weeks, to be with Kitty during her immunotherapy infusion sessions. Kitty's illness had developed into stage 4 melanoma and had spread to her lymph nodes, brain, and liver.

As Molly sat down in the waiting room, she saw Jane walking in from the infusion room. Molly stood up and approached Jane. Both women had tears in their eyes. They walked together out into the hallway. The two stood in silence for a while, heads down, staring at the floor.

"Jesus," cried Jane. She fought back her tears as she thought about her relationship with Kitty, their life together before Kitty's diagnosis of cancer. She'd always thought they were a perfect match. While they both were great athletes when they were younger, they had moved on to other interests. Yes, they ran together almost daily. Yes, they still were very competitive when they played their weekly Ping-Pong match. Yes, they still would go to ball games, eat hot dogs, and drink beer. But some of the best times they spent together were when they played music together.

Jane rediscovered her cello. Growing up in Stamford, Connecticut, every child who was anybody had to play an instrument. When high school athletics took a front seat, guess what took a back seat. Jane had been good, very good. Unfortunately, when her mom, the "other Doctor Brewster," died when Jane was fifteen years old, the cello was put away, not to be seen for decades.

Kitty had been a tomboy when she was a young girl. She could out run, out hit, out swim any boy her age. But when her grade school gave her a free violin and free violin lessons as part of the "Leave No Child Musically Behind" program, she took to it. Slowly at first, but this was different from all of her other activities. No hockey puck, no ball, no running involved. She was, if nothing else, persistent. She became quite an accomplished violinist. But when her father abandoned the family, the music stopped. Life got tougher.

Some parts of their pasts were difficult, but life with Kitty was anything but tough. Cohabitation suited Jane and Kitty. Jane loved to cook; Kitty loved to clean (if that was such a thing). Kitty started coaching girls' soccer. Jane coached girls' lacrosse. They went to each other's games. How great was it that they worked together during the day and supported each other at night. Jane and Kitty were true friends. And who is better to love with all your heart than your best friend?

Neither woman realized at first how their enjoyment of music together crept up on them. They began practicing, playing, practicing, playing, until they found themselves playing duets. They'd go to concerts together. They loved it. Vivaldi, Dvorak, Beethoven, Mozart, Tchaikovsky, Chopin. Hail to Itzhak Perlman and Yo-Yo Ma. It became one of their favorite things to do through good times, tough times, sad times, happy times, anytime.

She looked up at Molly. "Honestly, we loved our life together. But when Kitty was diagnosed with cancer, the music stopped again. The fun times turned into doctor's appointments, surgery, infusion days, and radiation sessions." Jane turned suddenly to face Molly.

"What sort of bullshit is this!" snapped Jane, face flushed, eyes swollen. "They have a nerve to call it a journey!" she yelled, fists clenched. "This is no journey. It's fucking *hell!* You want to see sadness? I'll give you sadness. You want to feel pain? I'll show you pain. You want to see going crazy, being lonely, having your heart broken, people falling through a hole to the other side of the earth and never hitting bottom? I'll show you it all. Dignity? Respect? Comfort care measures? Fuck that! This fucking sucks! God who?"

They stood in silence again.

"Y'know," said Molly, putting her arm around Jane. "We are told that music and art are about feeling. For as long as you and I can remember, the field of medicine has always been wedded to science. Science was always about numbers and calculations and objective observations and finding the best answers to the problem at hand. In the practice of medicine, the questions are always, "What are you thinking?" "What are you hearing?" "What are you seeing?" In art and music, the question is always, "What are you feeling?"

"Within the art of medicine and science, there deserves to be, and it's appropriate to have, feelings. Few of our colleagues in medicine give credence to having ups and downs of normal emotions. You and I, as physicians, are taught not to. It is a sign of weakness. It is all about scores on tests, measurements and studies, and results of experiments, but there are successes and plenty of failures, disappointments, and above all patients, people with lives, families, and souls. And it is normal and instinctual to feel happy, sad, sympathetic, empathetic, joyful, and angry."

"Got that right, "said Jane, letting out a big sigh. She looked down at the floor again in silence, wiping the tears away with her hands. "Look, it's been a long day. I've got to get home."

"Yeah, O.K. Take care."

The two women looked at each other with sad expressions, hugged again, and waved good-bye sorrowfully to one another.

***

Molly dried her eyes and walked into the infusion room. The lights were low. Soft music was playing overhead. Some patients had on headphones. She pulled up a chair next to Kitty's Barcalounger.

"Hey Kit, how's it going? Are you doing OK?"

"I'm O.K. As long as I don't die from the side effects the doctor told me about like colitis, hepatitis, dermatitis, hypothyroidism, or blindness" said Kitty.

"How's Aaron, and how's your research going? Got anything for me?" asked Kitty. She forced a smile.

"All is good," said Molly. "But as far as our work, Kitty, it's too early to tell." soon."

"Hope you hurry up," said Kitty. "I might need you."

Molly didn't respond. She grabbed her best friend's hand and held it without saying a word. She knew that her research treatments were not going to be available in time to treat Kitty, whose metastatic melanoma was one of the most vicious, fast-growing cancers. The only hope was that the combination immunotherapy would work, especially now that the melanoma had metastasized extensively.

Kitty broke the silence.

"I've got to confess to you Molly, sometimes I can be surrounded by people, and yet I still feel lonely. Truth be known, I have constant thoughts of death and dying, of my progressive disabilities, of my crumbling connections to friends and loved ones. And I can see sometimes how others often have a difficult time spending time with me, when that was never the case before."

"Well, whether you like it or not, you have Jane and I forever, sister."

Molly learned from her patients that they somehow knew how things were going to turn out, even before their doctor did.

"Hey, Molly, do me a favor, would you?"

"Anything, Kit.."

"Hang in there with me."

"Sure. Like I said, always and forever."

***

In August of 2015, Jimmy Carter, the 39th president of the United States of America, announced to the world that he had been diagnosed with malignant melanoma, an aggressive skin cancer, that had spread to his liver and brain. He was treated with surgery, radiation, and pembrolizumab, a new intravenous immunotherapy. This treatment uses the body's own immune system to kill cancer cells. Previous immunotherapies such as interferon and interleukin as well as chemotherapy had inconsistent and limited success, and most often produced results that were short-lived. At presentation, Jimmy Carter's prognosis was dismal. With the state-of-the-art immunotherapy treatment, he remained in remission without any evidence of melanoma present at seven years and beyond.

"I guess I won't be seeing a Jimmy Carter miracle, huh?" asked Jane after reading a news article about the former president. She was right. Kitty lived for another year. The immunotherapy looked like it was going to do it. But Kitty died one week before Molly and her team started their first human trials.

Molly had tried her best. She gave it her all as a practicing physician, as a researcher, to try to find the answers, and yet she had to say good-bye to her friend. The sense of failure, incompetency, of not being good enough, once again overwhelmed her. That same old feeling that physicians are trained to hold inside—the feeling of not having all the answers, that creeping sense of self-doubt, that feeling that you had to be perfect and make no mistakes, be strong—bubbled up and reminded her of why she worked so hard and with such passion.

"To be the real champion of the patient, you had to have real skin in the game," Molly had once said to Aaron. "Those feelings run deep. Empathy is real. The push to discover more, to push for the best and latest treatment available for the patient, one had to have one's heart and soul in the patient's outcome and possible cure."

Molly stood with Dr. Jane Brewster at the funeral. They cried together until they couldn't cry anymore. And then cried some more. As Molly stood there she thought, how can you be a champion of these patients if you don't love them? Yes, love your work, but also have a true love for the human beings you are trying to save … a recipe for pain when the patient was someone you loved.

And while Molly spent much of her time with cells and molecules, mice and chickens, it was the human spirit, the heart and soul of the human race, the cycle of life, that was the most important. She reminded herself of this each day with the family photos in her office, the poems in her desk drawer, and hugs from Aaron.

# Setback

Molly hired another Ph.D. scientist, Dr. Philomena Perez, two new technicians, and a new medical student Cynthia Goldman, following the debacle with Jeffrey Shaw. Molly and Takashi and the rest of the team had been working with their live nude mouse model for a good part of a year. They obtained human cancer specimens of all types from Dr. Samantha Patel and her surgical team, prepared them in the lab for transplantation, and carried out multiple experiments transplanting the cancerous tissue into the mice. Sometimes tumor cells were transplanted into the abdominal lining and sometimes directly onto the liver. The tumors would inevitably grow.

Dr. Norman R. Grist at Ruchill Hospital's Brownlee virology laboratory in Glasgow, Scotland, is credited with having discovered nude mice in 1962. This peculiar hairless mouse had a spontaneous deletion of a gene called FOXN1. Mice that have this specific gene deletion lack a thymus gland, have abnormal keratinization of hair follicles, and are immune-deficient (lack a well-functioning immune system). With no thymus, these mice cannot make T-lymphocytes, one of the key cells necessary to fight off foreign cells (including cancer cells). These mice are otherwise genetically and physiologically very similar to humans. Nude mice were the first immune deficient (immunocompromised and therefore a unique host within which cancer could grow without resistance) strain of mice to be used in cancer research. Because they are hairless, a tumor mass growing beneath the skin can easily be seen and studied.

In 1970, Dr. Beppino Giovanella, laboratory director of the Foundation for Cancer Research in Houston, Texas, recognized the potential of the nude mouse as a model for studying human tumor growth and suppression. A nude mouse can accept tissue grafts from a variety of species. Nude mice have remained the primary model for cancer research around the world for six decades. Molly's group found immediate benefits in using the tiny animals.

"I can't believe it," said Dr. Perez. "When the mice are injected with theobromine, the primary tumor soon disappears. This confirms the results we observed with our chicken experiments as well."

The team was delighted. They wrote several articles for medical publications, discussed their results at cancer symposiums, and were keen on moving forward with human subjects. Aaron worked alongside them, developing a formula by which theobromine could be given in a pill form.

"Aaron and I suspect there will be few side effects with the pill. We will be conducting further research to uncover why and how theobromine works to kill cancer cells," Molly announced to her team.

"Though nude mice normally have a lifespan of about six to 12 months, often they can be carefully treated and cared for in the lab, where they might live 18 to 24 months," said Philomena Perez. "After transplanting cancer cells into the mice, waiting for cancerous tumor masses to grow, and treating the mice with theobromine, various confirmatory experiments will then be carried out. Following these experiments, some of the mice will be sacrificed early, within days, some within weeks, and some within months, depending upon the experimental questions that we intend to ask."

***

Almost a year after starting the nude mice experiments, Molly's thoughts had already turned to preparing for human experiments. She was proud and excited about her results with mice. Theobromine had destroyed all the primary tumors that they implanted. She was so encouraged that she had even invited her mother to the lab in two weeks to show her the findings.

She and Philomena began their weekly review of the retained mice, those that were still alive at six, 12, and 18 months.

"Philomena," Molly called in a tone that made Dr. Perez hurry over to where Molly stood. "Look at number four, number seven, and number nine in this cage."

As the two women observed the mice, new bumps could easily be seen on the legs, backs, necks, and abdomens of the three mice. The two women quickly spot-checked several of the other cages. In each one, at least one mouse had acquired new tumors. All the mice that now showed new lumps beneath their skin were between six to eighteen months old.

Molly moved from cage to cage fighting back feelings of panic. Same sighting.

"How can this be?" she muttered, and then raced back to recheck each cage. "There must be a mistake."

"I am sorry, Dr. Moravian," Philomena said. "They were not like this two weeks ago. The tumors must have metastasized."

Molly turned pale, mouth agape, brow deeply furrowed. Molly and her team spent the next weeks sampling the new lumps. No doubt about it. The tumors in each animal, observed under the microscope, looked just like the original tumor cells first transplanted in the animals. Of the mice that recurred with tumors, less than 2% of them had any evidence of a tumor in the original site where their first tumor had been transplanted. The recurrent tumor masses had arisen in sites distant from the original site of cancer cell transplantation.

"The primary tumors were destroyed by theobromine," theorized Philomena to the group at their next team meeting. "But in some mice, certain cells must have broken away, perhaps before being exposed to theobromine, migrated through the bloodstream toward other body parts, broken through the walls of the blood vessels, implanted into distant tissues, and grown into new tumors. To repeat, despite theobromine."

Molly was aware of known data that showed that runaway cells could also occasionally circle back and start growing in and around the primary tumor as well.

"Let's get to work as a team and devise some tests to figure out what went wrong," she said. "What we'll do first is set up experiments giving higher doses of theobromine and administering the drug more frequently."

Some of the distant lumps got smaller, but most did not. In the meantime, more lumps appeared. Theobromine could not control the migrating cells from traveling to distant sites and implanting and growing in distant tissues.

Molly and her team worked day and night, practically sleeping in the lab, trying to figure out what went wrong.

"We have put our heart and souls into this project," she said to her team one morning, dark circles under her eyes, hair uncombed. "We cannot let this just crumble. I want you all to think about the process, question what happened, what have we learned, and come up with theories and solutions. We'll reconvene in one week. Leave no stone unturned. Read every published paper related to our situation."

The following evening, alone in the lab after hours, Molly knelt down to grab one of the mouse cages on a lower shelf. One of the mice escaped and jumped up onto the lab bench. Molly slipped to the floor, put her head in her hands, and whimpered. She did not have the emotional or physical energy to pursue the run-away mouse.

Susan Moravian entered the lab at that moment and saw her daughter crying like a baby. "Gib nie auf!" ("Never give up!") Molly looked up with fright. Her mother bent down, put her arms around Molly, squeezed her tight, and helped her up.

They walked into Molly's office and sat down. "Sorry," said Susan. "I got your email about how things weren't going so well. Want to tell me about it?"

Molly took a tissue, wiped her eyes, and blew her nose.

"I'm not sure what to do, where to start," she sighed.

"I do," Susan said. "I think it's high time you took a vacation. How ut a girls trip?"

Molly involuntarily started to object, to claim that the workload was too much for even a day off, much less a vacation. But then she reconsidered. At this point in the process, Molly had no choice but to rebuild anyway. So she decided that the whole team needed a breather. And she felt a need to reconnect with Susan, who had always been a source of strength and support.

"Thank you for being there for me yet again, Mom," she said. She hugged Susan.

"Give me a week to get things straight around here and you're on!"

# Mother-Daughter Vacation

Susan was an introvert. She was a certified public accountant with a solo practice, and she liked it that way. When not at work, she loved to curl up with a good book. Susan could spend the rest of her life reading endlessly in a room stacked to the ceiling with books.

She continued to practice some Jewish traditions and had a husband and family who were glad to follow her lead. She lit the Sabbath candles every Friday evening. But visits to the synagogue were infrequent. Religious school for the children was short-lived. She did enjoy the annual Seder, the traditional Passover dinner. Susan, Eddy, and their family would invite friends, both Jews and Gentiles, to share the story of the Jews' escape from bondage and some great matzah ball soup. Susan was guided by her mother Sadie's childhood experiences in Nazi Germany. "Never Again!" echoed in her heart and mind.

She had the best of both ethnic worlds because of Eddy's Armenian family. Christmas at Aram and Sonia Moravian's home was filled with heartwarming generosity. Susan particularly enjoyed havgtakhagh, the traditional Armenian egg cracking game at Easter.

Susan and Eddy brought their children up to be strong, flexible, focused, and goal-oriented. While there could be an intensity about the Moravians, they were not above having fun. So when she finally heard from Molly, it made her day.

"MOM, I haven't had a vacation in a year, and tax season is over now," Molly emailed Susan. "How about a girls' trip, just you and me? Somewhere warm. Talk to you later, love, M.O.M."

Susan loved getting emails from her daughter. Molly was good about communicating, whether she was at school, working, away in this country, or abroad. Susan would always sign her emails "Love, MOM."

Molly would sign off with her initials, "Love, M.O.M."

Molly had a half-day commitment at one of the annual oncology conferences giving a lecture at, of all places, the convention center on Jekyll Island, a tiny resort island, off the coast of southern Georgia. They would have the best part of the week to hang out together.

***

"How do you think the presentation went?" asked Susan, looking over their hotel balcony at the sand dunes, ocean grasses, and large expanse of Atlantic beachside. Mother and daughter had arrived on Jekyll Island the evening before, and Molly had presented her new research early that morning. Susan listened to her present her findings to her peers. She had never been so proud of her world-famous daughter.

"I thought other research scientists received it well," Molly told her, "even though I'm a woman." She smirked. "If you want to know a secret, I held back on some of our recent data that looks even better but is not yet confirmed."

"I thought it was great," said Susan. "It's unbelievable how close you may be to achieving a cure for cancer," said Susan. "I think what you've done is nothing short of remarkable," Susan continued. "I do have one question."

"Shoot," said Molly.

"I worry about your competitors. How does a person deal with venture capitalists, Big Pharma, fame seekers?" Molly's lips turned up, but the smile didn't make it to her eyes. "How about I answer that over drinks."

***

"Two dry martinis," the waiter announced in a long Southern drawl. He crept slowly along carefully balancing the drinks trying not to spill a drop while setting the glasses onto their table.

155

"Here's to my mother," said Molly, clinking glasses with Susan. They sat quietly for a moment, enjoying the warmth of the gin before Molly responded to Susan's earlier question.

"The way I see it, Mom, yes, I have developed something I believe is worth protecting. With my life, if necessary. But I can't put a playpen around it, can't swaddle it in warm blankets, can't build a fence around the yard like you did for me as a baby or as a little girl. I know the world is a tough place, and there are those who want things for themselves, not for me, not for the rest of the world."

Molly sighed.

"We have put strategies, behaviors, and systems in place to protect what is ours, but … I need to stay focused and keep moving forward." The furrow between her brows softened.

"This week, though," she said with a playful grin, "You and I are going to have the time of our lives!" She raised her glass.

"Cheers!" said Susan with a grin, and they clinked their martini glasses again.

*** 

Over the next few days, the Moravian girls got facials and massages together. They swam in the ocean and did laps in the hotel pool. They spent one whole morning ordering makeup online. In the afternoon, they biked around the island. They would sit on the beach and watch the squadron of pelicans flying in perfect formation.

Each evening, the women chose a different restaurant—pizza, steak, lobster, hush puppies. They walked the beach for hours and dined under the stars. And shop—did they shop! They checked out sun hats with twenty different hat bands, tried on costume jewelry, ate chocolate-covered pretzels and double scooped ice cream cones, tried on sundresses, and got matching flip-flops.

On their last night, the Moravian girls finished dinner at a beach-side café. They doubled their drink order and sat by a fire in their tank tops, shorts, and sandals. Later, they walked the beach with the towering dunes and held onto each other as they tried to keep their balance. They finally plopped down on the sand under the stars and discussed life, family, and motherhood. "

"I've noticed that your father is short of breath at times," Susan said. "It's probably nothing but, my daughter is a doctor."

"Mom, since when? I want you to keep an eye on that for me and let me know if it gets worse. Promise?"

"Promise."

"This week has been so much fun. So relaxing," Molly.

"Ditto. Let's walk further down the beach." Guided by the moonlight, they rose from the sand and walked arm in arm down the beach. They were giddy and laughing.

"Let's go swimming," Susan said impulsively. "There's no one here. We're both good swimmers. It's our last night. You know, just us Moravian girls."

"Mom! Are you crazy?" Molly giggled. "We don't even have our bathing suits!"

"What?" Susan said, flashing a sly grin. "What's so crazy?"

They looked at each other, hesitated, then stripped their clothes off and ran into the water. They splashed around, laughing and giggling, and ran out of the water. They struggled to put their clothes back on. The warm ocean breezes dried them off quickly. They walked back to the hotel holding hands. As they approached the wooden steps leading from the beach to the hotel, Molly turned to her mother.

"Love you, Mom."

Susan smiled.

"Love you too, Molly," and gave her daughter a big hug. Sandy and wet, they walked back to their room. How were they to know that they both had their shorts and shirts on inside out!

# Out of the Past

By the end of the next week, Molly and her fellow researchers had agreed on some theories and a plan of attack.

They gathered before a whiteboard that listed their observations and objectives.

1. Theobromine kills cancer cells, especially in the primary mass.

2. Theobromine must interfere in the gene that makes cancer cells grow and survive —Maybe?

3. Other cells, that perhaps have been unaffected by theobromine, (let's call them "spreader cells" or "escape cells" or "runaway cells") develop within the original cancer and are able to break through into the bloodstream, migrate down the blood vessels to a distant site.

4. The "spreader cells" must eventually adhere to the inside of the blood vessel wall.

5. These runaway cells must then escape out of the blood vessel, out into the tissues.

6. These escape cells must be able to establish themselves in the distant tissues and begin to grow."

"Possible plans of attack would be to:

1. Prevent these "escape cells from forming in the first place—-Maybe?

2. Prevent the cells from migrating through the bloodstream. —Maybe?

3. Prevent the "spreader cells "from adhering to the inside of the blood vessel wall just before they have a chance to sneak out of the blood vessel and begin to grow in the tissues. — Maybe?"

4. Prevent the cells that have gotten out into the tissues from implanting there.

"Further thoughts?" Molly's expectant gaze swept the room. "Thoughts?" she repeated.

"There has been some work in Japan using a common drug that eliminates stomach acid called cimetidine," Takashi offered. "Several labs have reported that cimetidine causes a decrease in the adherence of cells to the blood vessel wall. There are even some studies suggesting that some animals develop less metastases and even live longer with their cancers when treated with this or similar drugs."

Molly nodded; she had read about this work too.

"We still don't know why that works. But we are still not sure why theobromine works either at this point."

"This is not uncommon," Takashi added.

"We are working on these answers now," Molly said. These drugs *must* inhibit a gene or genes that the malignant cells need in order to grow, in order for the malignant cells to adhere to blood vessels, in order for them to break through the blood vessel wall and set up shop in the tissues."

Cynthia Goldman, the medical student whom Molly had recently offered a place on the team, spoke tentatively.

"So, you're saying that since metastatic growth is what kills these mice with cancer, if after destroying almost 100% of the original cancer cells with theobromine, and if we can then prevent the few spreader cells from causing metastatic disease, then we can prevent the mice from dying of cancer?"

"Let's hope so," said Molly. "Aaron spoke to Dr. Peter Bowman, the geneticist on the floor above us. He said that his team is ready to help and that he will be coming to talk to us next week about the genetic techniques we were thinking about using."

Molly and Aaron recently had a discussion about Peter's participation in their project and concluded that he had no involvement in the past thievery that had taken place.

* * *

Molly's team spent months setting up a multitude of experiments. Early one morning they gathered to brainstorm yet again.

"While we're all here this morning, Dr. Peter Bowman, our lead geneticist, wants to review a few things with us. Peter?"

"Thanks. Some basics now, so that as things get more complicated over the coming months and years, we'll all be on the same page. All living organisms are made up of cells. Within every cell there exist molecular materials, DNA, that make up the structure of genes. Genes code for the synthesis of proteins that tell the normal cell how to behave—how to develop, how to grow, how to reproduce, how to survive, and how and when to die."

Molly scanned the room Bowman had their attention. Good.

"Janet Rowley, a geneticist at the University of Chicago in the 1970s, convinced the scientific world that cancer was a genetic disease. That ran counter to prevailing notions at the time. So, as Dr. Rowley believed, we are going to prove that cancer is a result of specific genes being turned on or turned off or changed to an abnormal state in some way, causing the cell to no longer behave normally. By manipulating specific genes within these abnormally functioning cancer cells with specific drugs, we hope to cure cancer as we know it."

"Thank you, Peter," said Molly looking intently at the group.

"So let me be clear. We are on a quest for the Holy Grail—a cure for cancer. Make no mistake about it, we are not the only ones on this quest. Having said that, let's get down to it. Since the problem, as I see it, is that the spreader cancer cells sometimes escape from the primary cancer and travel in the blood system until they attach to the blood vessel wall. I think one key would be to try to prevent malignant cell adhesion to the blood vessel wall."

"Don't most oncologists feel that part of the success of chemotherapy has been timing?" Philomena asked. "If chemotherapy can be given soon enough, before the cancer has grown big enough or if given in a timely fashion following surgery, we often will get complete tumor cell kill, before any spreader cells develop and escape to distant sites."

"Right, Phil" said Takashi. "But in those instances where escaped cells *do* occur, I think options for inhibiting malignant cell adhesion to distant blood vessel walls is a good place to start."

"Takashi, would you mind giving the group your short but relevant review of blood vessel anatomy, again so we will all be on the same page going forward," asked Molly.

"Sure," replied Takashi. "Arteries are supple like garden hoses but, unlike hoses, blood vessels are made in sections. Think of a pipe-fitter welding short lengths into longer pipe lengths. Each section of pipe is called an endothelial cell. These endothelial cells are joined tightly together end on end to form one long artery so blood cells cannot seep out. The junctions between endothelial cells are called tight junctions."

"We think that cancer cells can float down, or migrate through, the blood stream and eventually adhere to the blood vessel lining. We have some very preliminary data that suggests if there is a significant number of cancer cells attached at a tight junction along the blood vessel wall, that cell density will cause the tight junctions to be not so tight. A space will then develop through which the cells are able to escape into the tissues. These escaped cancer cells will likely implant in those tissues and grow into a tumor at that distant site far from the original cancer mass."

"After reading the literature, particularly from Japan, suggesting that cimetidine, one of the first drugs used to reduce stomach acid, also has the additional properties of decreasing cancer cell adhesion, I looked into it," Aaron chimed in. He rose from his chair and headed to the white board.

"Cimetidine, $C_{10}H_{16}N_6S$, is officially N-Cyano-N'-methyl-N" - (2-{[(5-methyl(imidazol-4 yl) methylthio]ethyl} guanidine," he said as he wrote out the words. "Peter Bowman and I have been working remotely with Dr. Pierre Rodin at St Jude's Children's Research Hospital in Memphis, Tennessee."

"Dr. who?" Molly squeaked, almost falling off her chair. "Who did you say you were working with?"

"Dr. Pierre Rodin," Aaron said. "He plans to use the intravital microscope to test multiple drugs to see if we can block cancer cells from adhering to the blood vessel wall. I am betting on cimetidine. We will try to add a methyl group—CH3—to cimetidine to see if that might do a better job than cimetidine alone. It is well known that methylation of a gene (adding a methyl group, CH3) often inactivates the gene in question."

Thoughts of Dr. Pierre Rodin, the children, and the cocoa farms of Cote d'Ivoire flashed through her mind. How was he back in her life? How could she explain her first love to Aaron? But true to her calling, Moly stayed on task.

"If we're right," said Molly, "Cimetidine will be shown to inhibit the gene that encodes for the most important adhesion protein (the protein that makes cancer cells adhere to the blood vessel wall). If this is so, then Peter and Dr. Rodin are going to do some experiments where a gene can be made to fluoresce a bright color when activated. Dr. Rodin will send us videos. I hope we'll actually be able to see the key gene light up with our own eyes, the gene that's responsible for the spreader cancer cell's attachment to the blood vessel wall."

The excitement in Molly's voice was unmistakable.

"If we can then inhibit that gene from turning on by administering a drug, we prevent cells from attaching to the wall. We therefore prevent cells from getting through the wall, and thus prevent cancer cells from implanting in tissues and developing into a metastasis."

As they adjourned, Molly turned to her husband. "Aaron, could you get me the number for Dr. Rodin?"

"Sure," he said with a smile and a kiss. "See you tonight, honey."

***

With trembling fingers, Molly dialed the number.

"Bonjour," said Dr. Pierre Rodin.

"When the student is ready..." Molly whispered.

"...the teacher will appear," Pierre said, his voice choked with emotion. "Molly, ma chere I am so pleased to have this opportunity to once more work with you."

Pierre brought her up to date about how a change in government led to the clinic being closed and Pierre being forced to leave the country to protect his family. He had been able to plumb international connections to win a grant from the National Institutes of Health to study rural medicine.

"As you recall, the leading causes of death in my country were HIV/AIDS, neonatal disorders, lower respiratory infections and diarrheal diseases. Not surprisingly the American black population, less from genetics and more from institutional racism, stand a greater chance of being both exposed to those diseases and a lesser chance of finding adequate preventive care and treatment. I worked closely with the late Dr. Muhammad Qadri, who pioneered the work in intravital microscopy. It allows us to observe individual cells interacting in tissues while they are still in their natural environment, still in live animals or humans, at between one- and two-thousand times their normal magnification. This is a powerful tool that will help us figure out the biological processes taking place in live animals and the minute impact of environment in contracting and spread of disease."

Molly was impressed.

"When my friend, Dr. Qadri died, because of my success in funding my project and integrating his work into my research, I was named to replace him. Now this country doctor runs a major American medical research wing.

"You're far from a country doctor, Pierre," Molly said. Her head was still spinning. "I'm so happy. My search for a cure began in the cocoa fields when I asked you why—"

"I remember that," Pierre interrupted gently. "Did I not tell you that you will become a wonderful doctor?" he said. "You came to me a girl and left as a woman.

Molly's cheeks flushed as she remembered her time with Pierre.

"What shall I tell Aaron?" she blurted out.

"Tell him nothing," Pierre said. "This is your life now. I am happy to remain in your life as a friend and a fellow researcher. Beyond that, why create wounds where there is no need to do so? Sometimes, ma chere, truth is overrated."

It had been years since the miscarriage, years since she lost Pierre's baby. Should she tell him? Molly was about to speak, then thought twice about his words. Pierre was right. Aaron would be hurt by the news of her previous relationship with Pierre. And Pierre should never know about their child she lost.

# Hard Work Pays Off

Weeks turned into months as Molly's team worked on different aspects of the experimental project. Medical student Cynthia Goldman continued working on the nude mouse model. Her job was to deliver the drug cimetidine at different doses and different schedules to decrease metastases hoping the mice would live longer.

"I think that the way cimetidine works is that it obliterates the most important cell wall adhesion protein," she told Molly. "I think that the drug does this by inactivating the gene that makes that protein."

"We'll call it the ASK gene," Molly said. Members of the team looked confused. "What does that..." Aaron said, then turned red as he got it.

"That's right, Aaron, we're using your initials because you alerted us to the potential of cimetidine," Molly said. The rest of the team cheered. A few patted him on the back.

"Can I have your autograph?" joked Cynthia.

* * *


Aaron continued his work on making a new drug by adding CH3 to cimetidine. Philomena and Takashi used newly developed techniques, with Peter in genetics, to cut out specific pieces of genes and link fluorescent promoter genes to them. This would make the genes in question light up when activated.

Specimens went back and forth from Molly's lab in Boston to Pierre's lab at St. Jude's in Memphis and back again. With the use of Dr. Rodin's intravital microscope, the researchers were hoping to identify specific genes in cancer cells, manipulate those genes of interest, turning them on and off, and hoped to show how the malignant cells behaved in the bloodstream in the presence of cimetidine, methyl-cimetidine, and various other drugs and placebos.

Within months, data started trickling in.

"Our interim report shows that when our mice were transplanted with various cancers, the cimetidine-treated mice showed fewer metastases than the controls, and they lived longer too," Cynthia said during the morning meeting. "The higher the dose of cimetidine, the more successful we were at decreasing metastases and improving survival. We must still wait until all the mice die before we reach final conclusions."

"Takashi and I spent the last several months in Memphis, Tennessee, in Pierre's lab at St. Jude's," Philomena said. "We prepared nude mice in a similar way, as did Molly and Cynthia. Similar doses and schedules of cimetidine were applied to the subject mice. We were able to insert probes stemming from the microscope into blood vessels of the mice. The cancer cells were made to glow red. When cimetidine was injected, we noted that migration of cancer cells was slowed, but more importantly, cancer cells had a significantly diminished ability to adhere to the endothelial wall. Often, there was no adhesion observed at all."

Takashi nodded. "Higher doses of the drug showed enhancement of both these findings. Dr. Moravian, you will soon receive hundreds of videos taken of these events. And there's a genetic portion of this experiment that Peter will report on."

"I did most of the work here in my lab," began Peter. "But I spent the last few months setting up the final experiments in Pierre's lab. Through various genetic techniques, namely DNA microarray, CRISPR, RNA sequencing and Cre-lox recombination, we were able to label the six genes of interest."

Peter told how his team labeled the genes of interest within the malignant cells using fluorescent colors.

"When each of those genes was activated, each gene lit up with its own specific color. This allowed us to know which gene was the first to initiate the adherence of malignant cells to the blood vessel wall. The ASK gene lit up first every time. This gene is *the* gene responsible for initiation of adherence of cancer cells to the blood vessel wall. This is the one, Molly, that you had predicted."

Pierre, who was attending the team meeting by Zoom, chimed in.

"I will send you these videos for your review," he assured Molly. "I am now sending you, one of the most impressive ones, which Peter discussed just now."

Soon, up on the large computer screen in Molly's lab, the team clearly saw the malignant cells in red, magnified over 2,000 times..

"You will see the malignant cells traveling down the mouse artery, tumbling along," Pierre said. "Then you will see a bright burst of purple fluorescence when the ASK gene begins to activate. You can see the cells beginning to adhere to the blood vessel wall. As they gather, some cells are trying to push their way through the tight junctions in the blood vessel walls. You can occasionally also see some of the red cancer cells heaped up together outside the blood vessel wall within the tissues."

"Holy shit," murmured Takashi, "That is so cool."

"Finally, in the next video, after cimetidine has been administered, you can see an inhibition of all the cancer cells' activities," Pierre continued. "A slowdown in migration, little to no adherence, no cells squeezing through tight junctions, and no red cancer cells heaped up in the tissues."

"OMG!"

"Wow!"

"Unbelievable!"

"Great work, Peter and Pierre," Molly said smiling brightly.

"You will be receiving hundreds of videos from me for your review," Pierre replied.

"You all did a great job," said Molly.

"Totally. Good job, all of you," Aaron added. "On my end, I was able to add two methyl groups to cimetidine to make dimethyl cimetidine, a stable compound. We administered both dimethyl cimetidine and cimetidine in its usual form to specimens. It's still early, but it looks like dimethyl cimetidine outperforms the generic cimetidine."

Molly beamed. Months of hard work had finally paid off.

"From all of your hard work, an exciting picture is emerging," Molly said to the team. "It appears that in order to cure a patient with cancer, the patient might require a pill of theobromine, and a second pill of cimetidine … or dimethyl cimetidine? How much? How often? What are the side effects and toxicities? Much has been accomplished. I am proud of all of you. We still have a lot of work to do. Let's not let go of the tiger's tail. We'll meet again in two weeks."

# Betrayal

Dr. Charles Summer, administrative head of the Nott Science Laboratory for Cell Biology and Genetics on the Harvard campus, sat anxiously at his desk. Congressman William Fletcher, on the other end of the telephone, was lecturing him.

"So, Doctor Charlie, you do remember who obtained the money for that laboratory building of yours, don't you?"

"Oh, yes, sir," answered Dr. Summer, "and we do appreciate your efforts on a daily basis.

"Well, I have another opportunity for you to show your appreciation," Fletcher said. He and a venture capitalist were prepared to offer Dr. Charles Summer the chance of a lifetime. He would be paid handsomely, over a million dollars per year, to head up a laboratory in La Jolla, California. He would have the ability to recruit whomever he chose for a private cancer institute. He merely had to "borrow" the research that Dr. Moravian had been doing. Dr. Summer and his future colleagues would set up experimental laboratories, have free rein regarding recruiting and establishing contracts. The venture capitalist would do the rest.

This was the fourth phone call Summer had received from the congressman. After the third phone call, Dr. Summer called Dr. Peter Bowman into his office. After several long discussions, and after offering Peter the job as head scientist of the private laboratory and chairman of the genetics division, as well as the financial package of his dreams, Dr. Summer concluded by saying,

"After all, Peter, you do know Molly's entire operation virtually by heart, don't you? So I can count on you to make arrangements to obtain the necessary information?"

"No problem," Peter assured Dr. Summer. No more buying used cars, living in studio apartments, and no more cold New England weather. California here I come, Peter thought to himself.

***

Congressman Fletcher had worked with venture capitalist Ted Danzinger in the past. They had made some money together, but not enough. They came very close to making millions on a plastic formula they'd stolen from General Electric. This particular formulation of plastic, when melted into liquid form, reached the consistency of water. It could be poured into any mold. When this liquid plastic hardened, it had the strength of steel. The applications were limitless. It was a no-brainer. But something went wrong at the last minute, and their scheme fell through. Danzinger and Fletcher took a financial bath and were lucky to get out with their hides.

William, however, felt sure about this one. He called his good friend Raymond Dinunzio in Providence, Rhode Island. He saw to it that Ray did very well, thank you, with most of the construction outfits in New England. The senator wasn't sure whether he'd need a little extra muscle for this project, but he felt confident that Ray would be there if he needed him.

***

Ted Danzinger flew Dr. Charles Summer and Dr. Peter Bowman out to La Jolla, California. He wined and dined them. He showed them the site where the new cancer institute would break ground. Peter's excitement threatened to boil over. He would be making five times the salary he was making now and would have full rein over the hires in his lab. What else could he want?

When he got back to Boston, Peter fashioned an excuse to Molly about not being able to make the weekly meeting. He then called Molly later that afternoon,

"Hey, I know its late in the day, and most of your lab people are going home soon, but do you mind if I stay signed into the computer to finish up a few calculations."

"Sure, "replied Molly. "Don't forget to close out the computer and lock everything up."

170

"That was easy," thought Peter to himself.

When the lab had emptied, Peter rifled through Molly's emails and several years of previously published data. But other sections, her newest data, remained inaccessible without a separate password. Guessing, he tried some obvious combinations: CANCER, AARON, MOM, but without success.

He let Dr. Summer know.

"The congressman is desperate," Dr. Summers said anxiously. "He'll know what to do. Now leave quickly. Neither you nor I can be connected to this in any way."

* * *

"So, how was your appointment with Madame Curie, Golda Meir, and Lady Gaga all rolled up into one?" Sylvia Stein yelled into the kitchen as her husband of 35 years walked into the house.

"Not bad," Moishie said. "Three years and I got no evidence of cancer. She says I'm in admission." He smiled as he chomped on the end of an unlit cigar.

"That's *re*mission!" said Sylvia from the porch. "Well, whatever. She's one smart cookie. "

"I think she's got some kind of research goin' for a cure," said Moishie sticking his head outside onto the porch.

"She said something about human experiments. Tell you what. I ain't bein' no guinea pig."

"Yeah, well maybe she got yours early, and you're really going to be cured or somethin'," said Sylvia

"Yeah, but she still won't let me smoke my cigars.."

Sylvia was glad about the cigars. The house used to stink like hell. It was so nice when Doreen Verrecchia, her neighbor, was over the other day and the house smelled clean, not like a cigar spittoon. The two women were now sitting outside on their adjacent backyard patios after cleaning their respective kitchens, both with *mopeens* in their hands.

“So, Moishie’s doing okay?” Doreen asked Sylvia.

“Guess he got lucky that they found it early, and he got surgery, radiation, and chemo,” said Sylvia. “Yeah, it’s that guy, Eddy, who owns the luncheonette—his daughter. Brainiac, I hear. She fixed my Moishie up good. Very smart lady doctor. She’s discovering a cure.”

“No? A cure? That’s impossible.” Doreen clicked her tongue and shook her head in disbelief a few times. She turned toward the open door to her kitchen. “Hey, Vic, you ever run into that Eddy from the luncheonettes’ daughter?”

“Hey, gotta go” yelled Victor Verrecchia from the kitchen. “I might be a little late for dinner.”

“Where are you going?” snapped Doreen. “You never tell me where you’re going

“Aah, quit your bellyachin’,” Victor said. He left the house and got into his car. He lit a cigarette and took a drag. How is it that my wife is talkin’ about Eddy Moravian’s daughter? He thought. The Boss had just called him and told him to check out Eddy’s wife.

“You know,” said the Boss. “Find out what you can, Vic.”

Vic recalled seeing the daughter help Eddy with the racket years earlier. He had seen her hanging around the luncheonette a few times over the years. The Boss said something about maybe getting ahold of the mother’s computers.

***

Raymond Dinunzio, aka The Boss, was the head of the entire Cosa Nostra, the New England Mafia. He worked out of Providence, Rhode Island. Recently, the Boss got a call from a friend, the congressman, asking about the Moravian girl.

“Sounds like this senator got some info from the Congressional Appropriations Committee,” Raymond went on and on to Vic. “The ones that give the money to the National Cancer Institute scientists. Seems like there is a big hunk of money to share—the congressman, and some rich guy he’s workin’ wit think if they could get ahold of

172

this Moravian chick's scientific data—what they called intellectual property—they could get some of that dough?"

"A lot of the guys know her old man," cracked Vic. "Has a bookie joint in the back of his luncheonette, downtown."

"See what you can find out," the Boss growled at his underling. "Just a fact-finding mission. No rough stuff—yet. You get me?"

"Yeah, Boss. I'm on it."

"Geez," Victor muttered. "The Boss is always on me. So maybe I roughed up some people at times. So maybe I got a little aggressive at times. Not nearly as rough as my old man used to get with me for doin' nothin'."

Victor liked Eddy. He would work around the bookie if he could. Everyone liked Eddy. He knew Eddy's wife did the taxes for lots of his friends. He knew where to find her.

# Kidnapped

After stealing Susan Bloom's laptop from her office last night, and after reading through hundreds of emails, Tommy "Tech" Ragucci told Vic he couldn't pinpoint anything suspicious.

"Come on, come on," Vic yelled. "There's gotta be somethin'. Does she have a pet, her baby's name, her momma's middle name? Come on, you the tech guy—or aren't ya?"

"Nah, Man, I tell ya, nothing," Tommy whined. He knew he had to give Vic something. "But look, there is a lot of stuff between the mother and daughter, a lot of s science shit. And they sign their notes to each other 'MOM,'—like there was some sorta code or somethin'."

"So the doc's mom may have a few passwords, is that what you're sayin', Tommy?"

The Boss was breathing down Vic's neck. Vic knew what rolled downhill, which meant somebody with a lot of grease was shitting on the Boss to make him act like that. He knew he had to make something happen.

"Yeah, Vic, yeah," Tommy said.

"Pawn that computer shit," Vic said. "And keep your head down."

****

Victor was parked on North River Street on the east side of New Bedford. He had been there several hours, and it was now nearing 5 p.m. His car was in front of a small, one-story brick building that looked like it had been built in the fifties. A white sign hung from a post at the edge of the cement walk—Susan Bloom Moravian, CPA.

He'd been told to "investigate," so he was investigating. And if the mom was the weak link, he knew how to bring this investigation to a close—and get the Boss off his back.

****

Very odd, Susan Moravian thought when she got to work that morning and first noticed her laptop computer was missing. She thought she might have brought it home as she occasionally did. Susan even drove back home to check, but it wasn't there.

As she returned to her office she saw a black Lexus parked near the door. A man got out of the car and, moving with surprising speed, came up to her.

She gasped in surprise. He stood so close that Susan could smell the oily gel he used to slick back his long black hair.

"Who are you?" she demanded of the creepy guy, and when his only response was a smirk, she spat out, "Excuse me," and tried to push past him to enter her office.

"Get in," hissed the skinny little man in the black leather mid-length coat. The back door of the shiny black Lexus parked too close to hers was open, and he shoved her into the car.

He slammed the back door, and her stomach clenched as she heard the doors lock automatically. He scurried around to the driver's side, unlocked his door, and slid into the front seat.

"What do you want?" she demanded, sounding more confident than she felt as he shifted the car into gear. "Who are you? Where are we going?"

Tires screeching, they left the parking lot and pulled onto the Crosstown Expressway.

Susan noticed the wire mesh that separated the back seat from the front, like a police car. But this was no policeman. Her hands were trembling. Her heart was pounding. She took a deep breath to calm herself and thought of calling 911 on her cell phone. But he had snatched her purse away as he pushed her into the car.

"What is this all about?"

"Just cool it lady, or else."

Susan sank back into the seat and concentrated on remembering the route of the vehicle. The car meandered through downtown to the outskirts of the city, the rougher side toward the docks.

She could see no way out. She thought of somehow attracting attention—breaking the windows, screaming at the top of her lungs. But what if he had a weapon?

The car took several bumpy turns, going over roads with unending pothole after pothole, down by the old fish markets, and out toward the old fishing pier. It was now dark outside; she guessed they'd been driving for 30 minutes. Finally, the car stopped. It was pitch black.

The car locks popped open. The driver got out and opened the back door.

"Get out. And no funny business. I got something in this pocket you would not like to feel or hear," he said, sneering at Susan.

He shoved Susan forward toward an old, run-down building. Out of the dark appeared a metal door in the silhouette of the aged brick warehouse. He turned the knob, opened the door, and pushed Susan inside.

She stood in the dark, unable to see anything until her captor turned on the lights. Two overhead fluorescent lights came on. Susan could see the guts of an ancient, musty warehouse with hundreds of drum barrels of different colors, rusted, blackened, blue, white, smelling of oil and gas. A lone wooden chair sat under one of the fluorescent lights.

"Sit down, and again, no monkey business," Victor growled.

"You know my husband has ties with the police department and with some powerful characters in this city. If I were you I'd drive me home now."

Victor pulled out his hand gun, grabbed some black Gorilla tape off a dusty shelf, and walked toward Susan.

"Yeah, yeah. Now this isn't going to hurt a bit, as long as you do what I say. Put your hands behind your back." Susan did so. Victor wound the tape around Susan's hands and the back of the chair.

"Now," he said. "We're going to take this phone, call your daughter, and she's going to tell us all her passwords and codes for all the computer programs that involve her research." He shoved a cell phone next to Susan's right ear.

So that's what this is all about. I can't believe it, she thought. This horrible guy wanted to steal her daughter's research. There must be people way above this hoodlum's pay grade who want Molly's work.

"So, you think what you're after could be worth kidnapping me?" asked Susan.

"Oh, I'm sure of it lady," replied Victor. "Listen you, just tell me your daughter's number," said Victor impatiently.

"My daughter's research is locked up in a secret vault that no one has access to," Susan lied. "Not even her. It opens by an automatic electric mechanism twice a day."

"Sure, sure, lady. That's not what we heard." Vic knew she was lying. Peter Bowman, the scientist rat who was their inside man, had already described security at the lab. "Now, I don't have all night. What's the number?" He cocked his gun.

***

Eddy closed the luncheonette early that Friday, at 5:30. Guys had been coming in all day long, spending time in the back room. He finally got the last one out the door.

They had made reservations for dinner at the nicest restaurant in town, Tony Dimeo's, a little Italian place Susan loved, to celebrate their anniversary. The plan was for her to pick him up at 6:30.

At 6:45 Eddy started looking back and forth at his watch. He paced the diner and started rearranging cups and saucers. She was never late. He next looked at his watch at 7:15. He was worried. Eddy looked out into the dark parking lot. Nothing. He came back inside and wiped down the counter and all the tables—for a second time.

Eddy called her cell phone. Three times. No answer. That wasn't like her either. Eddy's thoughts were churning in all directions.

"What the hell?" said Eddy in a half-whisper, now feeling mid-sternal chest pain and finding it hard to breath. He had been coughing up blood lately but hadn't let anyone know about it. He had a business to run.

Susan would never be this late without communicating. Traffic jam? Car accident? He decided to call Molly. Before Eddy could say a word, Molly shouted,

"Dad, Dad, they took Mom. They kidnapped her!"

"Who? Who has Mom? What are you talking about?"

"I don't know," screamed Molly. "Some creepy guy called and said he had Mom and wouldn't hurt her if I gave them all my computer passwords. He wanted access to all of my research data."

Eddy had to think fast. Could this be true? What kind of guy would call and say that to Molly? Who would even think about kidnapping Susan?

"They wanted some passwords, Dad," Molly said. "They said something about hurting Mom and then just hung up."

"Molly, stay where you are. Give them what they want, only make a mistake with a few of them. I will make some calls and call you back shortly."

"Fine, I'll do what you say, Dad, but then I'm driving down there now!"

Eddy hung up. His breathing was tighter and his head was pounding. He ground his teeth and tears welled up in his eyes. No way he was going to let anyone hurt his soulmate in any way. Eddy took out two business cards from his wallet. He called the number on the first card.

"Bobby? Bobby Brown? Is that you?" Eddy asked the voice that answered on the third ring.

"Yeah, who's this?"

"It's Eddy Moravian. Down at the luncheonette. I think someone's kidnapped my wife. Can you come down to the luncheonette as soon as possible?"

Bobby was in the middle of supper, but he was already out of his chair when he quickly agreed.

"Sure, Eddy. I'll be down there in 10 minutes." Eddy hung up and called the number on the second card.

"Hello, who's this?" asked a woman's voice.

"This is Eddy Moravian. You know, down at the luncheonette? Is Moishie home?"

"Oh, Mister Moravian. You should be so proud. That daughter of yours is so wonderful—"

"Please, I'm sorry Mrs. Stein. I don't mean to be rude. It's an emergency. Could I speak to Mr. Stein, please?"

"Oh, oh sure," came the breathy response. "Here he is."

"Hello, Eddy?" said Moishie.

"Yeah. Listen, Moishie. I think someone's kidnapped my wife. Can you come down to the luncheonette? Now?"

Moishie had just finished eating the hot borscht soup and brisket that Sylvia had made him for dinner. He wiped the schmutz around his mouth with his napkin, threw it down on the table, and said,

"No problem. I'll be there in a jiffy."

Eddy hung up and immediately called Molly back. "Molly—"

"Dad," she interrupted. "I did what you said. This guy said he'd check it out with my 'friend' Peter in the lab and get back to me. That guy, Peter, his name is Peter Bowman. He must be involved in this. I can't believe it!"

"OK. OK," said Eddy. He paused to think. "I have help coming right now. We'll find Mom. If you speak to these thugs again, ask to speak to Mom. See if she's okay. I'll call you back soon. If you're driving down, meet me at home."

In walked Sgt. Bobby Brown with his partner, Sgt. Butch Duffy.

"Bobby, thanks for coming," Eddy said as he hung up the phone. "That was my daughter—she's worried sick. Eddy told Bobby the little he knew. Bobby asked all the usual questions about Susan as Sgt. Duffy listened and took notes.

"Butch, will you go back to the car and check this out?" Bobby Brown said to his partner."

"Sure, be back as soon as I can." The officer went out the door and into the night.

In walked Moishie Stein, chomping on a cigar, and followed close behind by "my associate, Rick Stiletto."

"Hey, Moishie, thanks for coming," said Eddy.

"What gives?" asked Moishie. He turned his attention to Bobby Brown, stared at Eddy, then back at Bobby Brown.

"What's he doing here?"

"Ditto," Bobby Brown said and sneered at Moishie.

"Look, I know this looks weird, but I need both of you," Eddy said. "I really need your help right now."

"You crazy?" said Moishie.

"Have you gone nuts?" Brown snarled.

"Look," said Eddy. "My wife has been kidnapped. It involves Molly's cancer research somehow. But we need to figure this out fast. I beg you …" Eddie's voice trailed off, and tears welled up in his eyes again.

Moishie coughed. Bobby cleared his throat. Silence followed.

"Look," Moishie said after a moment, "let me make a few calls. I'll be back." Rick Stiletto took a deep drag of his cigarette and followed Moishie into the back room.

"Look, I heard from the boys that Vic was tailin' Eddie's wife," Rick said when they were alone. "You know that guy, he can be a hothead. Goes off half-cocked sometimes. Gets aggressive when he shouldn't if you know what I mean."

Moishie knew Victor. He usually knew everything that was going on in New Bedford and the surrounding counties. The only time he didn't, and those times were infrequent, was when the Boss gave a private assignment to someone. So Moishie called the Boss and learned everything he needed to know in a few short minutes.

"This is not how I wanted this to go down," said the Boss. "I said nothin' about snatchin' the mother."

Moishie kept the frustration out of his voice as he reminded Raymond about his relationship to the Moravians, and about how Molly had saved his life. They talked a little more.

"This thing is going wrong ten ways to Sunday," said Raymond Dinunzio. "I don't like it. You know what to do, Moishie."

"I'll take care of it," Moishie said. He ended the call.

***

Sgt. Duffy was talking as he came through the door.

"Listen up," interrupted Moishie. "There's been a big, stupid mistake. Actually, it's one of ours. He's got his head up his ass. There's a story behind it, but no time for that now. I think I know where they are." He pointed to the officers and Rick.

"Let's all talk outside. We should be back soon, Eddy. You sit tight and we'll bring your bride back to you."

Eddy sank into a seat at one of the Formica-topped tables, drained yet hopeful.

The four men, cops and bad guys, filed out the door. They huddled in the parking lot for a few minutes, then split into pairs and headed for their vehicles.

Moishie, who knew all the places in New Bedford the boys would take people for protracted "discussions," led the way as the two cars drove toward the old fishing pier.

***

"She told you what you want to know, so let me go," shouted Susan.

"Look lady, I have had just about enough of your mouth. You give me any more guff you'll be wishin' you didn't."

"Do you even know what you're looking for? Do you even know what you're after with these codes and passwords you're seeking?"

"Take it easy. Don't get your knickers in a twist. We're gonna just wait right here until our friend Peter tells me that those passwords are

181

the real deal. They're all's what we need. Then, and then only, will I drop you back at your office. Then we'll all live happily ever after."

"If this Peter sold out my daughter, what's to stop him from selling you out too?

"Don't push me lady. My patience is wearin' thin with you. One more crack and I'm gonna have to hurt you."

"Big man. You're not smart enough or strong enough to hurt a fly."

Vic growled, "O.K. I've had enough of your mouth." He swung his arm to backhand her, then stopped suddenly as the door of the ancient warehouse crashed open.

Moishie Stein walked into the room.

"Well, if it ain't the Jew Man," Victor said with a surprise. "Fancy meeting you here."

Moishie stood silent as Ricky Stiletto walked through the door, followed by Sergeant Bobby Brown.

The thug stiffened, then pulled out his gun.

Moishie moved forward slowly, calmly, chomping more vigorously on his soggy cigar.

"Listen, shit-for-brains," he said, looking the younger wise guy straight in the eye, a curled lip revealing Moishie's clenched teeth.

"The way I see it, you've got two choices. You can put the gun down on the floor, untie Mrs. Moravian, get in your car, and take a drive to see the Boss right now, or you can get your head blown off by marksman Sergeant Duffy."

Vic wavered.

"Yeah," Moishie sneered. "He's right behind you who pointing an AR-15 assault rifle at the back of your empty skull as we speak."

Victor turned involuntarily and whack!, Moishie backhanded the thug, sending him to the floor. He looked up at Moishie with a blank stare. He looked at Sgt. Bobby Brown, at Rick Stiletto, and at Susan Moravian. He slowly turned his head to see Sgt. Butch Duffy in the corner against the back wall, sighting his rifle in Victor's direction with his finger on the trigger and a grin on his face.

Victor Verrecchia put down his gun, walked over to Susan, and removed all the tape. He walked slowly toward and through the doorway.

"And don't worry, we have your friend Peter in custody at the lab, so he'll be in safe hands," Bobby Brown said. "You'll probably meet him down at the lock-up tonight."

Vic walked out the door. Engines started. Cars drove away.

"I'm sorry, Mrs. Moravian," said Moishie Stein. "Are you OK? Your family is worried about you. We'll call and tell them you're okay. I need to take care of some things if you know what I mean. See you, fellas."

Moishie turned and walked out, with Rick Stiletto following right behind. Bobby Brown, pulled out his cellphone, dialed a number, stepped toward Susan, and handed her the phone.

"It's your husband and daughter, Mrs. Moravian. They'd love to talk to you."

"Mom, Mom are you safe?" shrieked Molly.

"Susan are you OK?" cried Eddy.

Susan let out a deep sigh. She snapped her head back, nose in the air, and said confidently,

"Damn right, I'm okay. Why wouldn't I be? It's our anniversary!"

# What Did You Learn?

Once Peter Bowman was apprehended, the entire underlying scheme was divulged. Her own colleagues, her trusted partners, the actual head scientist of the entire laboratory, had conspired against her. They tried to take away her life's purpose, her heart and soul. Pure greed. Evil personified.

Dr. Summer disavowed all knowledge of his and Bowman's activities, but a few months later he quietly retired. The congressman would successfully run for reelection in the fall.

Molly's *Zeyde* (grandfather), Julius Bloom, came to see them as soon as he heard what had happened. He had tears in his eyes as he hugged his daughter, Susan.

Molly, now seven months pregnant, was bloated, more fatigued than ever, and emotionally spent. With her mom home safe and sound and in the trusting hands of her dad, Molly and her grandfather decided to drive to the local zoo.

When Molly was little, her Zeyde Bloom would take her there every Sunday. It was a small zoo within a beautiful park. She loved the birds, the lions, the camels, and the zebras, but most of all, she loved the monkey house. Alice the Elephant came in a close second. As Molly got older, she would stand, holding her grandfather's hand, and stare at the monkeys for as long as she wanted. He never rushed her. Grandfather and granddaughter would walk and talk, asking and answering lots of questions.

Julius never failed to bring a book for them to read. He would always buy a chocolate bar for both of them and always gave her the bigger one. They would sit on a bench outside to read, or inside the main pavilion in inclement weather. At first it was the Doctor Seuss series, then funny children's poetry books, and next short stories and novels about girls and boys, but especially girls.

When Molly was ten years old, Julius brought *The Diary of a Young Girl* by Anne Frank. They took turns reading. Molly learned that Anne Frank died at 16 years old in Bergen-Belsen concentration camp in Germany. By the time she was 14 years old, Molly had reread Anne Frank's story 10 times over. She watched the movie with her grandfather at least that many times.

During these sessions, they would often laugh 'til they cried, but not infrequently discussions turned serious, and sad. Zeyde talked about his parents' lives in Germany through the Second World War. He told of fleeing the Nazis, running from safe house to safe house in a never-ending race for their lives. Julius would often explain his wife, Molly's *Bubbe* Sadie Bloom's, swimming prowess, her quiet but loving character, and her abandonment in war-torn Germany.

"Molly, my own parents were killed in Dachau concentration camp in Germany," Sadie Bloom told her granddaughter one day shortly before she died. "I am giving you this ankle bracelet and locket that I have worn since I was a little girl in the old country. It represents your heritage."

* * *

They walked in silence to the monkey house.

"Zeyde, the world does not always have my best interest in mind," Molly said.

"Not everyone will have our daughter's best interest in mind. I see now that not only do we have to struggle to produce something good and noble for all humanity but we need to protect ourselves, if not fight back, against those who seek to get ahead at any cost."

Julius pulled out a chocolate bar for Molly and opened one for himself.

"Molly, do you know what you said to me when you were 10 years old after we finished reading Anne Frank for the first time?" he asked. "You said, 'Gee, Zeyde, she didn't even get a chance to make the world a better place.'"

185

He paused.

"So, you get back in the ring and finish what you're doing. Make the world a better place for that beautiful daughter of yours who is going to arrive on earth before you know it."

They stood together, staring at the newborn chimpanzees, savoring every last bite of their chocolate bars.

Molly's grandfather had lots of lessons to teach. When things were not going well, when some unfortunate situation had occurred to upend Molly's life, the one piece of advice that always came through would begin,

"Well, Molly, there is only one question to ask yourself here." Patting her shoulder and with a knowing smile he'd ask, "What did you learn from this?

"Explore that question, and you'll find solutions. When you learn from unfortunate situations, you won't let them happen again. And you can take that to the bank."

# Toward the Finish Line

"Listen up, everyone," Molly said as the team assembled for their weekly research meeting. This meeting was different, though; they would discuss the next phase of their research projects without the presence of Dr. Peter Bowman. Each team member expressed how sorry they were about Susan's ordeal and how happy they were that Susan had survived the debacle unscathed.

"We will go through everything separately, discussing each essential part of our theory, but I wanted to just give a simple overview of where we have been and where we are going."

"First, I'd like you all to meet Dr. Bruce Jordon, a brilliant geneticist, the newest member of our team."

Bruce was one year ahead of Molly in medical school. He was African-American, short, stocky, and would sit up front at every class with his heavy, black-framed glasses, always knowing the answer to any question that the professor asked. He was one of the... no... was *the* smartest student in the class. He went on to be a brilliant geneticist and was sought after by laboratories throughout the country.

"He has come across town from Tufts University, to work with our team. We are lucky to have him. We will have further introductions after our meeting today."

"Welcome."

"Hey, Bruce."

"Nice to meet you Dr. Morton."

"Hello."

"Alright, to move forward, first, we all know that from our *in vivo* mice and chicken data, theobromine destroys most, if not all primary tumors in animals. Through years of brilliant work, Bruce in his lab, as well as our own cell biology team, have now shown that a heretofore unknown gene, which we've named Molly's Team gene, or MT gene for short, mutates and can cause any normal cell to convert to a cancer cell. MT gene is necessary and sufficient for any cancer to initiate, grow, and develop. Almost by working backward, our team has shown that MT gene is theobromine's target. It is theobromine's ability to suppress the MT gene that in turn suppresses any initiation, development, or growth of cancer."

"Second, we know that it is possible for malignant cells to escape from the primary site, usually before we diagnose the cancer, and travel via the bloodstream to distant body sites. We know that these escaped cells must first adhere to the blood vessel wall in order to thrust themselves through the wall and set up shop in the tissues outside the veins and arteries. We have now shown that dimethyl cimetidine eliminates this process by suppressing the function of the most vital adherence gene, the ASK gene."

Many of the researchers in the meeting smiled, and a few turned to look at Aaron.

"Third, going forward, we will try to show that there is a yet-undiscovered gene that is necessary for any and every malignant cell to implant itself in tissues. We intend to show that there is an effective drug that is able to suppress what we're calling the implant initiator gene. This would inhibit any malignant cell from implanting, growing and developing at a distant site. Any questions?"

Dr. Rodin, attending the meeting via Zoom, spoke up.

"I just want to know, were you crazy enough to review all those videos that I sent you and count all those millions of cells? There must have been over 500 videos."

"Well, it helped me to get through the morning sickness each day," said Molly, and everyone laughed. "As I watched those cancer cells travel down the bloodstream and adhere to the blood vessel wall, I observed that approximately 100 or more cells had to congregate and adhere to the blood vessel wall at a single site before one of those cancer cells was able to push through the tight junctions, into the tissues, and implant and grow and develop. As it turns out, if less than 100 cells adhere to a single site, the chances of one of those cancer cells getting out of the blood vessel was less than one percent. So there seems to be a numerical threshold somehow, wherein cells are able to adhere, implant, and form metastases."

"So, if theobromine and dimethyl cimetidine are able to keep this magic number below 100, and hopefully way below 100, we can prevent metastases from forming. And if we stop metastases from forming, we can prevent death from cancer in the majority of cases."

"But what if some cells actually get through, despite our two-drug cocktail?" Takashi questioned.

Takashi continued. "We all know now that as we examined our mice at 12, 18, and 20 months out, treatment with theobromine kills the primary tumor, and dimethyl cimetidine treatment prevents runaway cells from adhering to the blood vessel wall. Unfortunately, there are still some animals, perhaps less than two percent, that develop metastases. Why?"

"The answer is because some cancer cells, despite our efforts, somehow get through the blood vessel wall and initiate implantation, growth," Molly answered.

"So how do we prevent this? What is the ultimate imitator of implantation in human beings? How do we investigate this? What models can we use? Take it away, Phil," said Molly, turning to Philomena with a smile.

"So Molly suggested that we concentrate on the point and time of cell implantation," said Philomena Perez. "We talked about the ultimate normal human implantation experience, i.e. human embryo implantation in the human uterus. What gene(s) control this? What proteins? What makes this process a success or failure? What gene ultimately initiates this process? So, we discussed a possible model, possible experimental strategies."

Philomena continued. "Greater than eighty percent of the time, failure of the embryo, the blastocyst, to implant is the most common reason for human pregnancy loss. Lots of mouse and rabbit genetic studies have been done, and we reviewed these exhaustively. Many genes have been shown to be importantly associated with human embryo implantation. However, as best as we can tell, no one gene has yet to be designated as *the* initiator—the very first gene that must get activated in order to turn on all the other genes responsible for completing the process of embryo implantation. If we can nail down that initiator, we could find a way to inhibit that specific gene activation. And therefore, inhibit implantation."

"You got it exactly, Phil. Let's take a break, finish our work for today, and reconvene tomorrow to discuss the set-ups, the goals, and….," squeaked Molly. Molly looked surprised for a moment.

"Oh, sorry, the baby was just kicking again."

Molly was in her ninth month of pregnancy and would be out of action for a while. She wanted to make sure that work at the lab would continue smoothly in her absence. She had already set up multiple desktop computers and two laptops at home to communicate with the team from her home office.

# The Final Assault

At the follow-up team meeting the next day, everyone stood around Molly holding steaming cups of coffee as she addressed the group briefly, then turned the discussion over to Cynthia.

"OK," Cynthia said. "We know that there are a number of genes involved in human embryo implantation, like p53, p72, muc-1, and mdm-2. We also know that at the very millisecond that implantation into the uterus occurs, genes of both the uterine cells and the embryo activate seemingly at the same time. We hope to prove, that the *very first* initiator gene comes from one of the embryo cells."

"In order to do this, let's talk about an animal model for our implantation studies."

"Dr. Moravian suggested using the European rabbit, *Oryctolagus cuniculus.* We'll be aiming to identify and then regulate the implant initiator gene; that is, we want to turn it off and on at will. Using the techniques of hysteroscopic visualization, poly-nucleotide specific fluorochrome studies, and intravital microscopic videos to visualize the nuclei of cells in the rabbit embryo, we'll obtain data to pinpoint the initiator gene of the implantation process."

"We have obtained the consent from 50 women involved in the hospital's IVF program, and our project got the green light from the Investigational Review Board. Published data has shown that when "good" embryos fail to implant during IVF, the most common cause is an embryo gene malfunction. Using the information from our rabbit model, we will show that we can turn off the key gene that initiates implantation in humans."

Molly chimed in. "I am betting that the same genes that are involved in rabbit embryo implantation are also the key to cancer cells implanting in human tissues. If so, we hope to show that there is a drug that can permanently shut off the cancerous implantation process in humans. I have some ideas regarding possible drugs, one in particular that I have in mind. Bruce?"

"The p53 gene and the proteins it encodes are involved. The normal p53 gene is well known as a human cancer suppressor gene. When normally activated, it plays a role in keeping humans from developing cancer. Many human cancers, however, have been found to have a suppressed or deactivated p53 gene. A situation where p53 gene is turned off, tends to promote cancer growth."

"The P53 gene has been shown to be involved in normal implantation and has been shown to promote apoptosis, programmed cell death. Turn on p53, and we'll see acceleration of cancer cell self-destruction, as well as suppression of the key gene responsible for implantation of cancerous cells."

"Our strategy would be to use a drug to turn on and then continuously maintain normal activation of the p53 suppressor gene. This will continuously suppress the key gene needed for cancer cells to implant, and voilà! A combination of three effective, relatively non-toxic drugs that act synergistically. A cocktail to destroy cancer cells at every turn."

"In many cancer patients," said Molly, "the p53 gene has been found to be turned off. We hope to show that Suberoylanilide hydroxamic acid, SAHA, a histone deacetylase inhibitor, will likely turn the p53 gene back on and keep it on. This is an oral medication with manageable side effects. I suspect it may *also* suppress the growth of the primary tumor and the migrating cells trying to adhere to the blood vessel wall, at the same time it is suppressing the implantation process."

While Molly spoke, the team was simultaneously watching a video, on a large screen in the lab, of an embryo implantation on the uterine wall of a rabbit.

"Pierre," said Molly with alarm. "Play that video back again, slowly."

"I keep seeing the same fluorescent colors over and over, on each video we've taken," said Pierre.

"Wait, there, see that?!" Molly's voice rose in excitement. "See that tiny flash of yellow just before all the other colors start to pop?"

Pierre replayed the video.

"Oh my God! There it is! I see it! A tiny yellow flash right before all the others," he said.

"No doubt about it. It appears that as the embryo implants go on to the uterine wall, a number of fluorescent colors shine brightly. These represent activated genes cascading to allow the embryo to implant onto the uterine wall. But just a millisecond before all those genes are activated, this one key gene, the yellow one, is turned on, presumably promoting or inducing all the other genes that are necessary for implantation, growth, and development of the embryo at that site in the uterus."

"Right," said Molly. "That *is* the implantation gene we've been looking for, the initiator that begins the implantation process, the gene we hope to suppress if we want to inhibit cancer cell implantation."

"Now that we can recognize it, we'll need to make sure the gene signal is coming from the cells that are trying to implant and not from the uterine wall cells receiving the embryo for implantation. We'll have to prove that when cancer cells invade into the tissues, the very first and necessary gene that gets activated comes from a mutated gene indigenous to the cancer cells, not the tissues. If that is so, then the gene we want to inhibit is that very implantation gene in the cancer cells. When we turn off that implantation gene continuously, cancer cells will not be able to implant into tissues and grow and develop into metastases. The patient will not die of their cancer."

"This is great," Dr. Rodin said, talking rapidly, giving a thumbs up and looking over to the geneticist. "Bruce and I will talk with our biomedical engineer and the rest of the team. We'll set up the final experiments based on this concept."

Molly listened intently, but at the same time she was also sensitive to her body's signals. Lately she'd been feeling kicking on a regular basis. She was happy for every uncomfortable kick and hoped and prayed that the baby would be normal. After all, she was a physician; she knew all too well what could happen. Was the baby going to be healthy? Would there be complications with the delivery? Was she going to love this baby? Was this baby going to love her? Would she be a good mother? Would the work in the lab go O.K. without her? She'd soon find out.

# A World Worth Living In

Molly finished breastfeeding and placed the baby in her crib for a nap. Exhausted, she plopped herself with a thud into a deep armchair by the bay window of their new home in the Boston suburb of Brookline, Massachusetts. Looking out to the backyard on this late spring morning, she stared at the new bird feeders that Aaron hung. She was struck by the glowing yellow of the American goldfinches, the shyness of the suet-loving pileated woodpeckers, and the way the male and female cardinals protected each other…never very far away from one another. This nature observance expanded her reverie to questions as to what kind of planet her daughter would inherit.

Aaron quickly passed by Molly, sitting in the den, with a basket full of laundry, stopping to plant a quick kiss on the top of her head.

"I've got several errands to do after I finish grocery shopping," said Aaron.

He had been so happy when Alexandra was born. When it was time for him to leave the hospital after ten hours of sitting by his wife for the delivery, he raced home to get some sleep, only to be pulled over by the state police for going twenty miles over the speed limit. When Aaron, with tears streaming down his face, began telling the female trooper how happy he was to be a first-time father of a beautiful baby girl, the officer let him go with just a warning. Aaron thought that he could see some moisture in the trooper's eyes as she turned and got back on her motorcycle.

While Molly could think of nothing but the miracle of her baby girl, there was a restless piece of her thought process that was drawn back to the laboratory. She was conflicted as to her desire to go back to work at the moment. She of course communicated with her lab remotely over the last many months. How can I ever go back and leave this princess? she thought. It seemed like the world had stopped to make way for this beautiful human being. Molly wasn't sure the earth would start spinning again. And what kind of world was this child being left with? What environment would she fall heir to?

As Molly heard Aaron's car pull out of the driveway the phone rang. She arose from the armchair and walked over to the kitchen table where her cell phone vibrated across the slick surface.

"Hey, Molly, how are you doing? How's the baby?" said Dr. Bruce Morton, the team geneticist. Molly's face brightened at the sound of his voice.

"Just great," said Molly. "She's sleeping now."

"Hey look, Molly, I know you are a bit busy being a new mom and all, but I just thought you might like some news from the lab, an update. By the way, you know that we're all so happy for you. Take all the time at home that you need."

"Bruce, so great of you to call," said Molly. "So what's up?"

"Well," said Bruce, "We completed all the mice and rabbit projects. You're going to be happy. I'll give you the bottom line."

"The rabbit uterine fluorescent gene studies continue to consistently show a separate and consistent blip before every other flash is seen. This of course means that this new gene that we found *is* the initiator of the entire implantation process. Then we ran the same fluorescent gene studies in culture dishes with embryo cells only and repeated the experiments with uterine tissue cells only. This showed that the key initiator implantation gene definitely comes from the cells trying to implant, and not from the cells in the tissue that are receiving those cells."

Molly drew in a deep breath and let it out slowly.

"Sooooo, suppress the human implantation initiator gene and we should be able to suppress the malignant cells from implanting," she said.

"We did all the experiments again with the drug SAHA on board," Bruce continued, "both in the rabbits and the mice. SAHA prevented implantation. None of the mice that were transplanted with cancer showed evidence of implantation, development, or growth in a distant site. No metastases.”

“So, bottom line,” he said, “We’ve discovered a new gene that initiates implantation … at least in the mouse and the rabbit. We’ve proved that we can turn this gene off and keep it off with our drug. When the animals are given the drug, no implantation takes place. We hope the same genetic process is applicable to humans.”

Molly didn’t know what to say. Her heart was fluttering, bursting with pride and gratefulness. Her animal work had reached the peak of its success. They were ready to move on to human trials. She gave a huge sigh.

“You all did a great job. Thanks. We are fortunate that it worked out,” said Molly.

“We’ll publish our results, and let’s meet on Zoom to start planning our Phase I, II, and III human trials. Thank you for calling. Much appreciated.”

For the first time since the baby was born, Molly truly felt like she had her “work” hat back on.

“Wait, Molly,” Bruce interjected before Molly could hang up. “One more thing. The team got together and decided, no argument please, that we call the new gene, M.O.M. And we won’t let you object.” Molly was silent. She was flushed. Her eyes welled with tears of gratitude. Finally, she said, “Thank you. Love to the entire team. Talk to you soon. Good-bye.”

Molly stood in the kitchen staring out the window for a long while.

***

When human cancer drug trials are initiated, there are generally three phases that are pursued following successful animal trials. The goal of Phase I trials is to determine the correct dose and frequency of the new test drug that can be safely administered to patients with acceptable toxicity.

The goal of Phase II trials is to treat patients who have different types of malignancies. The question to be answered is which, if any, of these kinds of cancers respond to the new treatment.

The goal of Phase III trials is to use the new drug to challenge the best-known therapy to date being used to treat that particular malignancy. If the new drug successfully treats that specific cancer, say lung cancer, and shows results that are better than the previous best treatment for lung cancer, then the challenging cancer drug henceforth may well become the new best choice for lung cancer therapy.

Successful Phase III trials often achieve FDA approval for that new treatment. Unfortunately only a small percentage of drug trials actually succeed, despite years of effort, hope, and scientific valor.

***

Molly anxiously went to work several weeks later. Over the next few months, there were international publications and speaking engagements. Human studies were designed and initiated. Phase I studies established the dose and frequency of the three-drug cocktail—theobromine, dimethyl cimetidine, and SAHA. There were very little toxicities or side effects. In the Phase I trials where only the most advanced patients were treated, most lived much longer than expected. So far, Phase II studies have been successful as well. Patients with every and all cancers responded. Their cancers went away, and in most cases, stayed away. Most patients, particularly the patients who religiously continued to take their three-drug cocktail twice a day, remained in remission.

"It's quite miraculous," said Molly to her team at their weekly meeting. "Three oral drugs, with little in the way of toxicity. So far, patients with every type of cancer that we've tried have improved dramatically, to the point where their cancers have receded, and so far, have not come back." She beamed at each smiling face in the room.

"Granted, the patients have to take their medications twice daily, and may have to take these drugs for the rest of their lives," Molly went on. "Please continue to keep all of your records neat, accurate, up to date, and transparent. I will be reporting our results at several international oncology conferences this year. I will need to refer to all of our data thus far. Please continue to work on our publications, and again, as always, stay true to our data, report only what happens, no more, no less. I will review all of your papers next week, no matter what stage of writing you are in at that point."

The oncology world was starting to take notice: Molly's name, laboratory results, and human trials were raising eyebrows. Oncologists and cancer researchers were excited but were already demanding confirmatory studies. Phase II and III human trials had years until completion.

***

As the months flew by, Aaron was promoted to a full tenured professorship in the division of biochemistry at MIT. He was busy with several exciting projects going on in his lab, while Molly was of course back in her lab 24/7.

Then there was Alexandra Victoria (AV, for short) who was growing, moving, exploring. She was a breath of fresh air for both Molly and Aaron at the end of the day. Molly could not watch her enough, talk to her enough, teach her enough, share with her enough, read with her enough. Alexandra was now a year old.

"You know," Molly said one evening, "with our work, we have brought our daughter into a world that will be a better place. We will share our sense of purpose with our children. Hopefully, the world will be recipients of their accomplishments as well."

She and Aaron chatted while Alexandra sat on Molly's lap blowing kisses to her dad. She struggled to get down and crawl.

"Children?" said Aaron. "Did you say, children?"

"Yes," said Molly with a smile. "Now please put AV to bed and meet me in the bedroom. Sooner rather than later, please!"

* * *

As Dr. Molly Moravian's Phase II and III human trials proceeded over the next several years, it was becoming clear to the national and international oncology community that, having been sought after for centuries, a *cure* for cancer had arrived. Maybe? However, time after time, at lectures describing her new anticancer regimen, Molly received mountains of pushback from her mostly male colleagues. From the audience, in the hallway, in emails, on social media, and in international medical journals came questions that implied,

"How could this be? A cure? Impossible. And the leading author and researcher is a woman?"

Questioning a breakthrough like this? Now that *is* and *should be* the norm. It certainly was fair game to query the data, the materials, the patient cohorts, the calculations, the study designs. But while Molly and her team received praise and encouragement from her women research colleagues, it seemed that a predominance of her male scientific competitors appeared less interested in the science of it all and more interested in challenging her motives, integrity, or truthfulness in research. There were those who no longer made eye contact with her in the hallway or in the cafeteria.

One day, Molly showed Philomena an article from a magazine about how sexism crippled a renown scientist's career.

There have been hundreds of brilliant, renowned scientists during the last several centuries. Among those scientists that are most recognized by the general public are Madame Curie, Louis Pasteur, Albert Einstein, Jonas Salk, and the team of James Watson and Francis Crick. The latter two were, of course, the team that unraveled the secret structure of DNA, the essence of genetics.

There have been giants, well-known to most in the scientific field, who have not been as publicly famous. Some of these brilliant men and women have indeed lapsed into obscurity for one reason or another. Greed, power, envy, politics, unfair competition, and misogyny would be but a few of the reasons for these unsung heroes to have been forgotten.

In the late 1940s and early 1950s, a scientific war raged in the quest for the chemical structure of deoxyribonucleic acid (DNA). The battle was being fought by many prestigious laboratories throughout the world, including those of Dr. Linus Pauling (California Institute of Technology) and Dr. James Watson and Dr. Francis Crick, of the Cavendish laboratory, Cambridge University. Another laboratory working on this problem was that of Dr. Maurice Wilkins at King's College, London. As competition heated up in 1951 and 1952, Watson had a meeting with Dr. Wilkins, who took the liberty of showing Watson and Crick some stellar work that was being conducted by Dr. Rosalind Elsie Franklin in her laboratory. He specifically showed them photographs (particularly the vital photograph number 51) of her work with X-ray crystallography and X-ray diffraction, without her permission.

This technique allows the scientist to pass X-rays through proteins in crystallized form. This produces hundreds of patterns that help decipher the molecular makeup of said protein. At age thirty-one, Franklin used this technique to discover the chemical structure of DNA. She had not yet chosen to share *her* discovery with the outside world. Very soon after the Watson-Wilkins meeting, Watson and Crick, on February 28, 1953, announced to the world that they had determined the double helix structure of DNA.

The molecule DNA is encoded with the genetic information of all living things. Crick was rumored to have said, "We found the secret of life." Rosalind Franklin was not included in the announcement. Watson and Crick never gave Franklin credit for *her discovery*. In 1962, Watson and Crick as well as Wilkins won the Nobel Prize in Physiology/Medicine. Dr. Franklin was ignored. In 1968, James D. Watson wrote a book titled *The Double Helix*. He explained how he and Crick had unearthed the set of genetic instructions held within the cells of all organisms, and how these instructions could be passed from generation to generation. Again, no mention was made of Dr. Franklin's contribution. She dropped into obscurity, only to develop ovarian cancer, and died in 1958. Nobel prizes are not awarded posthumously.

"It's as if our discoveries have made other researchers jealous, even angry," Molly said to Philomena.

Skepticism and accusations were not uncommon when she lectured at national oncology conferences. Leaders of major laboratories, mostly men, aggressively questioned her results. Molly would answer these attacks by encouraging others to reproduce her work, which would invariably confirm her findings. Indeed, studies were being done worldwide to support (or refute) Molly's team's findings.

"It's so frustrating," said Molly to Aaron. "We women have fought systemic bias for years. Women have had to punch our way through sexist attitudes, men feeling like they're the only ones who can be smart, talented, unbeatable. It's pure envy. You know I'd be the first to acknowledge a mistake, a flaw, a crack in our methods, our results."

***

The oncology community the world over finally came around. Disclaimers, doubts, and repeat trials turned into stories of success. Time and time again, Molly's data held up to intense scrutiny. Though the world at first could not believe that a major killer could now be cured, her decades of hard work definitively showed this scourge on the planet to be dissipating.

A lethal disease that refused to ignore any family in the nation, the second most common killer of Americans, would now be a thing of the past. Oncologists, patients, scientists, and the media were simply awestruck. To the medical world, it was a dream come true. A brilliant woman and her team of scientists had conquered the highest peak.

More importantly, they opened the door for future geniuses, future innovation, future ways to do it better, do it simpler, safer.

"Don't forget, we have a big day tomorrow," Aaron said as Molly lay in bed reading a treatise.

"Really? What? What's going on?" asked Molly.

"I don't know how you could possibly forget," said Aaron. "The FDA will be making a decision on your cancer cure. I guess we'll have to go to bed with our fingers crossed, our toes crossed, and our legs crossed."

"Well, maybe the fingers and toes," said Molly." I'm not sure about the legs."

# The Noblest of Prizes

Molly was trying to get the girls on to the school bus on time. Her now-graying hair was tousled, pulled back in a loose ponytail secured with a red scrunchie. She still had her nightgown on under her thigh-length blue alpaca sweater.

Her daughters were very excited to go to school today. More than usual. Alyssa had her third-grade Halloween parade, and Alexandra had her fifth-grade parade. Alyssa was a shiny green dinosaur with a big long tail that she kept tripping over. Alexandra was dressed as a mermaid. Her coconut bra kept slipping, and her blue sequin flipper kept twisting around and getting stuck in her *Wonder Woman* backpack. Molly kissed the girls and helped them onto the bus. Her cell phone rang as the bus drove away.

"Is this Dr. Molly Moravian?" asked the male voice with a Swedish accent.

"Who is calling?" asked Molly, walking home, waving to the girls on the bus.

"I represent the Nobel Committee in Stockholm, Sweden. You have been selected as this year's Nobel Laureate in both Physiology or Medicine *and* Chemistry. Congratulations. You will be awarded your Nobel prizes on December 10 in Stockholm. Further information and instructions will be emailed to you in the near future. Again, congratulations. We look forward to seeing you then. Good-bye."

Molly hardly had time to say thank you before the caller hung up. She could hardly breathe. She dialed Aron's number as she walked into the house.

"Hello. Molly?"

"You are not going to believe who just called me!"

***

Every scientist and physician seated in the ornate and crowded Stockholm Concert Hall would tell you the award presentation that day was for *the* greatest scientific achievement the world had ever known.

Sitting among hundreds of attendees at the Nobel Prize Awards ceremony, Molly felt surreal, as if in a dream, as she listened to the distant, slow cadence of the presenter. Molly could feel the intense heat from the bright lights of the enormous chandeliers hanging from the gold leaf dome above and all eyes were upon her.

"We are in awe and honored to bestow these Nobel Prizes to the only person to have achieved the Nobel Prize in two different fields simultaneously in the 130-year history of these awards. The only other woman to have been awarded two Nobel Prizes, Madame Marie Curie, received the Nobel Prize for Physics in 1903 and the Nobel Prize for Chemistry in 1911. Only three other individuals have been awarded two Nobel prizes."

"Not even Einstein," whispered Aaron who sat by her side.

Molly's gaze swept over those in attendance bedecked in glittering gowns and handsome tuxedos with starched white shirts. She glanced down at her marine-blue floor-length gown, chosen to match her sparkling eyes. She was uncomfortable. Not only did the spaghetti straps dig in and her newly dyed-to-match flats pinch her toes, but her dress was a little too tight to go unnoticed.

The pageantry, the excitement, the history, the grandeur. It was a bit overwhelming for a girl from an old crumbling town in New England. She heard the presenter use words like brilliance, greatness, genius, world-renowned, impossible-made-possible, but that's not what she felt in her gut.

Why me? she thought.

She had concluded her Nobel Laureate's lecture the day before by saying, "I planted a seed, not knowing or understanding what it might bear, what fruits of scientific discovery the resulting plant would produce."

"That plant was staked by my friends, family, colleagues, and by my research team that is the epitome of persistence toward honesty and truth. All the hard work and resulting discoveries were fertilized by my heritage, my ancestors' bravery and strengths.”

“Those who came before me gave me the confidence, fortitude, curiosity, and relentless drive to succeed. From this nurturing emerged a gift for all mankind. I hope that gift is used wisely.”

Molly grinned as she thought back to that lecture. At that moment, she had been unable to think of anything but the people in her life who helped her get to where she sat at that very instant.

She closed her eyes and thought of her mother, Susan, shouting in German, “Gib nie auf!” (Never give up!)

Then there was Aaron, her courageous, loyal, brilliant husband.

And she thought of her dad, Eddy. She was a bookie’s daughter, raised by a father who skirted the law but never skimped on love.

And who was that out there in the audience? The wizened old man clenching an unlit cigar in his mouth looked just like--Molly bolted upright as Aaron elbowed her in time for her to hear her name:

“...and therefore, because of her aforementioned astonishing achievements, the Royal Swedish Academy of Sciences has awarded this year’s Nobel Prize in Physiology or Medicine for discovering the root cause of all cancers, *and* the Nobel Prize in Chemistry for discovering the cure of the same, to Doctor Molly Olivia Moravian.”

# Family Matters

Molly and Aaron decided to splurge and sail on a liner back to the United States. It was everything they hoped it would be. One night, as Molly strolled the deck, she walked toward the group of chairs that her family had claimed during most of the voyage.

There was someone wrapped in a blanket sitting in one of the chaises. Molly was disappointed that she wouldn't be able to sit in her usual chair. She walked past the night owl, a little man, his woolen Scottish cap pulled down over his eyes, smoking a cigar.

"I must be crazy," Molly murmured. "That sort of looks like Moishie Stein."

She made an about-face and walked slowly back toward the occupant of "her" chaise.

"Hey, how you doin', Dr. Molly?" the familiar voice greeted her.

Molly couldn't believe it. Moishie Stein on board?

"Moishie, is that you?"

"Yeah, and I'm still smokin' my cigars too," came the gruff response.

Molly gasped. Her eyes popped wide open. "Moishie, excuse me, but what are you doing here?"

"Well, I heard about this prize thing, and I didn't see how I could miss it," Moishie said, chomping on his cigar.

She was incredulous.

"Moishie, what are you talking about? And again, what are you doing here on this ship?"

"When a man is proud of his family, he's gotta show up and support them," said Moishie, eyebrows raised, a slight grin across his face. He puffed on his cigar.

"What?" asked Molly, brow furrowed, eyes squinting.

"Listen, Dr. Molly. You better sit back in your chair and let me tell you a little story." He sat up straighter and pushed the blanket down to waist level. Molly sat back in her chair and fixed her gaze on the wizened old man.

"Look, when WWII was over, we all just wanted to get out of there and go home. Aram Moravian went home to Watertown to his cute little Armenian wife. He wanted to start a family. Me, I came home to nothin'. My family was dirt poor. I had no money, and I was a bit of a wise-guy. I was lookin' to get married, same as all the other guys. Her name was Sonia. A nice Armenian girl. Cute. Quiet. Plenty of tragedy in her life. I got hooked up with the wrong bunch. I got some money in my pocket, wore a few suits, and next thing you know, Fingers Filano wants me to go down to New Bedford to work the rackets with him down there. So off we go. Pretty soon, my wife gets pregnant. We have a little boy. But I was a bum. I was a lousy husband and a worse father. So, one day when the kid was about six months, I just up and left. A real scoundrel. I felt real bad about it."

"Meanwhile, Aram comes home to his bride in Watertown. Very soon after she gets sick. Real bad. Next thing ya' know she up and dies on him. Long story short, I got him fixed up with my ex that I had abandoned. Who woulda' known? They married and raised that little boy. We went our separate ways. And we stayed that way."

Molly sat frozen in the chair next to Moishie, tears rolling down her face.

"Moishie, are you telling me what I think you're telling me?" Molly asked in a soft whisper.

"I think so," replied Moishie with a warm smile.

"My father, Eddy, is your son? And you are my grandfather?" Moishie looked up, glasses at the end of his nose, cigar dangling from his lips.

"I'm afraid so, Dr. Molly."

Molly couldn't catch her breath. A million scenes flashed through her mind.

"Don't get me wrong. Aram has been a good grandpa to you. He has done all the right things. And your Grandma Sonia has been there by your side from the day you were born."

"A few years later when I smartened up a bit, not much, I met Sylvia down at our local watering hole. Waitin' tables, cracking her gum, smokin' her cigarettes 'til the ash fell off in your lap. She didn't have nobody. Her whole family--parents, brothers, sisters, aunts and uncles-- all got wiped out by Hitler's boys. She still has that number tattoo thing on her wrist. So, we got married. Neither of us wanted kids. We both thought we wouldn't do so good at it anyway."

"Sylvia's been good to me. She's put up with a lot of my stuff."

Molly did not know what to say. She was flustered. How could this be?

"Does my father know all this?" Molly blurted out.

"Yeah, well I guess so. I had a discussion with him before we left the States. Sylvia put me up to it. She said that since you cured me of the big one, she figured it was about time I told you and him. Can you believe how lucky I got, a bum like me, the day I found out that Eddy had come to New Bedford and was runnin' the luncheonette?"

"So that's why you—"

"He's my boy," Moishie said, "so I looked out for him. You gotta problem with that?"

"So what did my father say when you told him?" Molly managed to ask.

"Well, you know Eddy. He let me off easy. In a nutshell he said, "Welcome to the family. And then he convinced me that I should go to this cancer prize thing."

Molly was breathing hard, and the tears were still flowing. She moved closer to the little man on the next chaise and held his hand tightly.

"Regrets? Oh, yeah. I thought of coming out with this thing many times. But I didn't want to screw up the one good thing I did in my life."

Molly and Moishie sat there without talking.

Moishie broke the silence."

"I'm honored that you're my granddaughter."

"I'm honored that you are my grandfather. I wish I had known a little sooner. But hey, by the way, what about that large diamond ring in the red velvet box that was left on my bureau that time we got robbed?"

"Oh, yeah, well, I wanted to get you something good, on account of, you know, we're related," explained Moishie. A soft chuckle.

Silence again.

Molly got up slowly, kissed Moishe on the top of the head and began to walk away. She turned back toward the little old man and with a big smile, said,

"Hey, grandpa, see you around. Thanks for sharing."

"You bet," said Moishe as he exhaled a puff of smoke and pulled the blanket up to his chin.